CU00642470

CONTENTS

This Book Belongs To :— ....

....

Original edition published 1955.
This facsimile edition printed by Leo Paper, China.
© 2004 Express Newspapers, London.
All rights reserved.

RUPERT

A DAILY EXPRESS PUBLICATION

06665   Printed in England

4'6

RUPERT and POLL

RUPERT STOPS TO LOOK

*" My pals are staring at the tree !
I wonder what it is they see."*

*The chums say, " We can't see from here,
But Rastus noticed something queer ! "*

RUPERT is coming home from the shops when he sees his pals near a tree. "Hallo," he says, "I wonder why they are staring up into the branches. I must go and see." As he turns to cross the grass a little cat scampers up to him. "You're a pretty puss," says Rupert. "Where have you come from and what's your name ?" The cat purrs and rubs against Rupert's legs, and the little bear stops for a moment to stroke the friendly creature. Then he hears his chums talking among themselves and he hurries on to join them. The little cat runs after him, and then leaps up the tree, soon disappearing amongst the leaves. "I wonder what he's after," says Rupert, "and what are you all gazing at ?" "Rastus *thinks* he saw something brightly coloured up there," says Edward, "but he's not sure about it."

PARROT

On the next eight pages are small pictures of the Guides signalling a message to you with semaphore flags. Each signal stands for an alphabet letter. If you are unable to read the code message, turn to page 107.

RUPERT CALLS EDWARD BACK

As Edward Trunk goes on his way
The little bear calls out, " Please stay! "

" There's something up there all the time,"
Says Rupert as he starts to climb.

"Ah, well," adds Edward, "we must get on with our errands now. Perhaps Rastus was dreaming!" "It wasn't a dream—I was wide-awake," insists Rastus. "I certainly did see something and it seemed to be hopping from branch to branch." "It might have been a bit of coloured paper blown about by the wind," laughs Edward. "Come along. We can't stay here all day." They all turn away, but Rupert still peers up into the branches of the tree. Suddenly he sees a flash of colour high in the tree-top. "Hey, Edward!" he cries, "I can see it too! Do come here!" Edward runs back, and they both gaze excitedly. "I think I could get up this tree if I could climb on your back," says Rupert. So, while Edward stands very steady, Rupert balances carefully on his pal's shoulders and manages to reach a branch.

RUPERT COAXES THE PARROT

Gasps Rupert, " Fancy seeing that !
A parrot, sitting near a cat ! "

" Look, here's a biscuit," Rupert cries,
And to his hand the parrot flies.

" I wish that I could stop and play,"
Says Edward, " but I mustn't stay."

And at the gate stands Mrs. Bear,
Who says, " Now what have you got there ? "

Up and up goes Rupert and suddenly, straight in front of him, he sees the little cat sitting on a branch, close to a brightly-coloured parrot. " So it was a parrot we saw," he cries, " and he's certainly good friends with the cat ! This is a queer business ! " He quickly climbs down and tells Edward all about it. " I'm going to try to get him down," he says, taking a biscuit from his bag, and holding it out. Sure enough, the parrot flies down for it and perches on Rupert's arm quite comfortably, while the little cat clambers down the tree to his friend. " Oh dear ! It's time for me to go," says Edward, and sets off alone, while Rupert takes the parrot back to his house, with the cat following. Mrs. Bear meets them at the gate, and soon gives him some more biscuits for the bird. " Now I must find who owns these two," says Rupert.

RUPERT LISTENS WITH PAULINE

" Perhaps he'll talk—I haven't tried,"
Says Rupert to Pauline the Guide.

They listen while Poll clicks away,
And wonder what he wants to say.

" He doesn't talk—he clicks in Morse !
That's what the noises mean, of course ! "

" Let's ask my friends. Maybe they'll know,"
The Girl Guide says, so off they go.

As Rupert turns away he meets Pauline the Guide. She is very eager to hear the parrot talk. " Let's give him a bit of biscuit," she adds. " Perhaps he'll say ' thank you '." But the parrot eats his biscuit without a word, then flies to the branch of a nearby tree and begins to make queer clicking noises. " How funny he is," laughs Pauline, and then stops suddenly. " Listen ! " she cries excitedly, " is it——? Yes, it *is* ! " " Is *what* ? " asks Rupert. " What are you excited about ? " " Why, you listen to the way he clicks with his tongue ! " cries Pauline. " It is just like a message in Morse code." Rupert is very surprised. " Then what is he saying ? " he gasps. " Well, I can't quite make it out ! I'm not very good at Morse," says Pauline, " but the other Guides may know. Come on ! I know where to find them."

RUPERT HEARS THE MESSAGE

" *Well, that's a thing I'd like to hear!*"
Laughs Beryl, " What a strange idea!"

" *Keep still,*" *says Rupert, " then you'll see*
The parrot will fly down to me!"

They all sit quietly on the ground,
And listen to the clicking sound.

" *It's really Morse code!*" *Beryl cries,*
And reads the words in great surprise.

Before long Pauline is telling her story to Beryl and Janet. " What a crazy idea! " laughs Beryl, the eldest of the three, " who ever heard of a Morse parrot? Let's hear him." So Rupert holds out some more biscuit to the parrot, who has perched on a nearby tree. The Guides keep quite still, and in a moment the parrot is flying down towards them. " You certainly love biscuit, old boy," chuckles Rupert, as the bird settles on his arm and nibbles the piece. Directly he has eaten the biscuit the parrot begins clicking away, and Beryl jots down everything the bird says. Soon she has writter a number of dots and dashes, and then she jumps up, looking very astonished. " You're right! " she cries, " These clickings make real words! Listen! " and she reads out, " VIGO, ADEN, GOA, S.O.S., RIO! "

RUPERT REACHES THE SHACK

" Maybe a sailor owns this pet,"
Says Janet, " We may solve it yet ! "

Up Rupert jumps, and off he strides,
" Sam's sure to know," he tells the Guides.

" Sam isn't home to-day, I fear,
It looks as though there's no one here."

Nearby a window's open wide,
The pets now disappear inside.

"Well, this *is* a queer business ! " cries Rupert. " Let's see what we can make of it ! " They murmur the strange words aloud, and then Janet suddenly says, " Those words are nearly all the names of sea ports ! This parrot may belong to a sailor ! " " Right ! " says Rupert, jumping to his feet. " Then we'll ask Sailor Sam ! He's the only seaman round here." He leads the way to Sailor Sam's shack. The little cat runs along beside him, and the parrot flies overhead. But when Rupert reaches the shack, no one answers his knock. Suddenly he hears a scratching sound, and, looking round, he sees the cat scrambling up to an open window, through which the parrot is flying. " Well, they seem at home here," he cries, " they must belong to Sailor Sam." " Janet's idea was certainly right ! " exclaims Beryl.

RUPERT FINDS SAM IN BED

" I'm sure that someone must be there.
Let's knock again," says Rupert Bear.

" Please lift me to the window sill !
I'm going in—perhaps Sam's ill ! "

There, in a bunk built in the wall,
Lies Sam, not looking well at all.

" Poor Sam is really very bad ! "
Sighs Rupert, looking rather sad.

"Where is Sam ?" murmurs Rupert as he knocks again. He and the Guides wait awhile, listening carefully. "Come in !" says a weak voice from inside the shack, but when Rupert tries the door, it is locked. "This is rather worrying !" he frowns. "If only I could climb through that window !" "That's easy !" says Janet, and, lifting him up, she helps him scramble over the window sill. Inside the shack,

Rupert finds Sailor Sam lying in a bunk built into the wall. "You *do* look ill !" he cries, and explains why he has come. Sam gives a weak chuckle. "Been practising my Morse," he whispers, "couldn't manage bigger words— such a long time since I used it—parrot must have mimicked me ! Oh dear ! I do feel bad ! It's my old complaint again !" Rupert, feeling very worried, opens the door and tells the Guides.

Rupert and Poll Parrot

RUPERT HUNTS FOR DR. LION

" I'm certain that it would be wise
To fetch the doctor," Beryl cries.

" We'll find the doctor soon," they say,
" If each one goes a different way."

Cries Rupert thankfully, " Hurrah !
I'm sure that's Doctor Lion's car !"

" Our sailor friend is ill," says he,
" So, Doctor, will you come with me ? "

"There's only one thing to do," says Beryl as Rupert finishes his story, "we must go and fetch Dr. Lion at once ! But he will be on his rounds now, so there is no knowing what part of the village he may have reached. We had better go in different directions, then one of us will be more likely to meet him." Quickly she gives her orders, and Rupert and the others run off. The little bear dashes down the hill and into the village at top speed. Suddenly, turning a corner, he sees a car ahead of him. "I do believe that's Dr. Lion's car !" he gasps. "I must hurry, or he will be off to another patient !" He gallops along the road for all he is worth, and as he draws closer, he sees Dr. Lion coming out of the house. "Thank goodness I have found you," cries Rupert, and gasps out his story of Sailor Sam's plight.

RUPERT RIDES WITH THE DOCTOR

Off drives the doctor, very fast,
And Pauline sees the car rush past.

The doctor hurries up the track
That leads him to the sailor's shack.

" I'll feed the parrot and the cat,
I'm very glad I thought of that ! "

" He can't be moved—he must lie still,"
The doctor says, " he's very ill ! "

Dr. Lion listens carefully. "Hum ! I must see him at once," he says. " Jump in, Rupert ! " As they drive off quickly Rupert and Pauline catch a glimpse of each other, and the Guide runs to tell her chums that the doctor has been found. Dr. Lion drives as far as he can, and then Rupert leads the way to Sailor Sam's shack. As they get near the house the little cat runs to meet Rupert, looking very pleased to see him again. Rupert takes Doctor Lion straight to Sailor Sam's bunk, and while the doctor examines him Rupert hunts for some food and feeds both the parrot and the cat. When Dr. Lion has finished, he turns to Rupert. " It's lucky you fetched me, for Sam is very ill," he says. Rupert soon explains the whole story. " It was all because Poll Parrot had learned to click his tongue in Morse ! " he chuckles.

RUPERT'S CHUMS AGREE TO HELP

" I hope that we aren't very late,"
Says Beryl, running to the gate.

" The nurse will find us jobs to do,
And we can run the errands, too ! "

Sighs Rupert, " How relieved I am
That, thanks to you, we've found poor Sam ! "

So each of Rupert's pals decides
To do his best to help the Guides.

The Guides have arrived, and Rupert runs on ahead of Dr. Lion to tell them the news. " I shall send a trained nurse," says the doctor, " for, even if Sam could be moved, the hospital is full." " Oh, do let us help ! " cries Beryl eagerly, " We can run errands to the village and we can help the nurse, too." The idea pleases Dr. Lion, and with a kindly nod he returns to his car and drives off. " That's fine ! " says Beryl, " we shall all be able to do our good deeds for many days ! " " You have done one already," smiles Rupert, " for you recognised Poll Parrot's Morse, and that led us to Sailor Sam." Then he runs to tell his pals all about it. " There's a grand job for us to do," he says. " While the Guides help the nurse we can take care of Sam's pets and tend his garden until he is well enough to get up ! "

HOW TO MAKE A PAPER CAT'S HEAD

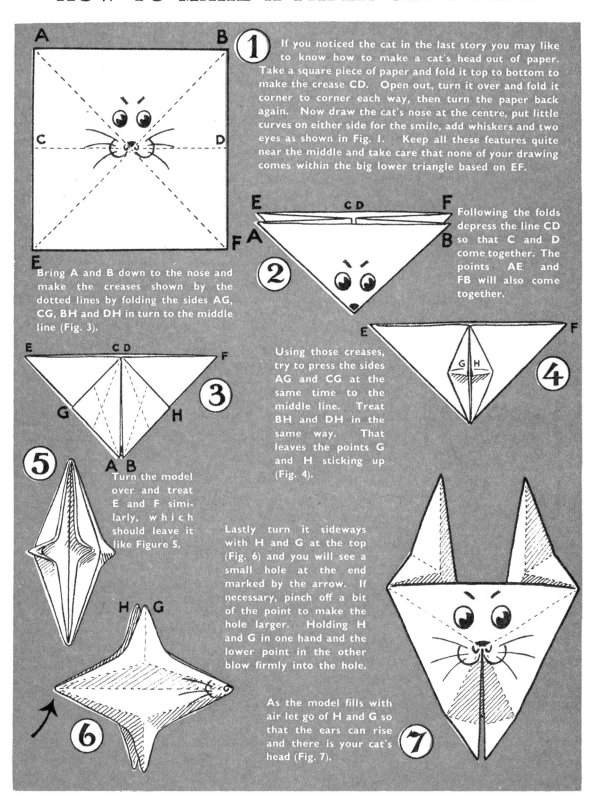

1 If you noticed the cat in the last story you may like to know how to make a cat's head out of paper. Take a square piece of paper and fold it top to bottom to make the crease CD. Open out, turn it over and fold it corner to corner each way, then turn the paper back again. Now draw the cat's nose at the centre, put little curves on either side for the smile, add whiskers and two eyes as shown in Fig. I. Keep all these features quite near the middle and take care that none of your drawing comes within the big lower triangle based on EF.

Bring A and B down to the nose and make the creases shown by the dotted lines by folding the sides AG, CG, BH and DH in turn to the middle line (Fig. 3).

2 Following the folds depress the line CD so that C and D come together. The points AE and FB will also come together.

3 Using those creases, try to press the sides AG and CG at the same time to the middle line. Treat BH and DH in the same way. That leaves the points G and H sticking up (Fig. 4).

4

5 Turn the model over and treat E and F similarly, which should leave it like Figure 5.

Lastly turn it sideways with H and G at the top (Fig. 6) and you will see a small hole at the end marked by the arrow. If necessary, pinch off a bit of the point to make the hole larger. Holding H and G in one hand and the lower point in the other blow firmly into the hole.

6

As the model fills with air let go of H and G so that the ears can rise and there is your cat's head (Fig. 7).

7

RUPERT'S WILD FLOWERS PUZZLE

"Tra, la, la! It's a lovely day!" Rupert sits up with a start at the sound of a merry little voice. Peeping round the tree-trunk, he is astonished to see three tiny gardeners working amongst a patch of wild flowers. Can you name the eight kinds of wild flowers shown in the picture? The answers are given on page 107.

RUPERT'S
CHRISTMAS DECORATIONS

Your Christmas tree will look very pretty if you follow Rupert's idea of making your own decorations. Candles, lanterns, baby crackers and other gay things can be made from oddments which you will find in the house.

BUTTON

SILK TASSEL

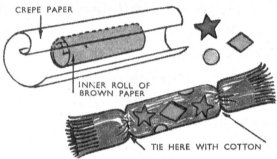

CREPE PAPER

INNER ROLL OF BROWN PAPER

TIE HERE WITH COTTON

Baby Cracker. Roll a strip of brown paper into a thin tube 2 inches long and gum the outer edge to keep the paper from unrolling. Cover the tube with a piece of coloured crepe paper which should overlap the tube about 1 inch at each end—a touch of gum will keep the outer covering firm. Make the "waists" of the cracker by fastening cotton just beyond the ends of the inner tube. Cut fringes at the edges, then decorate the cracker with tiny shapes of coloured paper cut from sweet wrappers.

Dwarf Lantern. Cut four pieces of paper $4\frac{1}{2}$ inches by $1\frac{1}{2}$ inches and two pieces of card 2 inches square. Colour the strips of paper and pleat them. Make a tassel with short lengths of silk thread, and fasten it through the middle of one piece of card. Sew the button to the centre of the other card, leaving a loop to attach to the tree. Paste the ends of your pleated papers to the cards to form the walls of the lantern.

Tree Tassel. Fold three or four coloured sweet-wrappers together to make a narrow strip, then fold the strip in half and fasten a loop of thread round the folded part. Snip the ends to form a fringe which can be spread out, as shown.

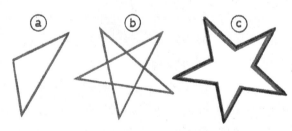

(a)   (b)   (c)

Tree-top Star. Make a card triangle about three times the size of that shown in fig. (a). Cut it out and use it as a pattern. Place it on a piece of card and draw round it in three different positions so that you draw fig. (b). Now cut round the outer lines shown black in fig. (c). To decorate the star you can either paint it a bright yellow or gum silver paper on to it. Gum a loop of paper to the back of the star so that it can be hung on your tree.

Sparklers. Find five coloured metal milk-bottle tops and make a small hole in the centre of each. Push a match-stick through the holes, as shown, and fix each top with a blob of gum. Hang the sparklers on your tree and they will glitter in the light.

MATCH-STICK

LOOP OF THREAD

BEAD

MATCH-STICK

PAPER TUBE

MILK BOTTLE TOP

COTTON WOOL

FINISHED CANDLE AND HOLDER

Elfin Bell. A metal milk-bottle top can be made to the shape of a bell by moulding it on a thimble. Remove thimble and trim edges of bell. Thread a small bead and sew it inside the bell as shown, leaving a loop of cotton at the top.

Fairy Candle. Push some cotton-wool in the end of a thin paper tube about 1½ inches long. Gum the wool in position and twist one end to form a " wick ". Fit a match-stick through the centre of a milk-bottle top, as shown, and gum it into the cotton-wool.

SHAPES GUMMED BACK TO BACK ON THREAD

Paper Chains. Some small coloured paper shapes are gummed back to back on a length of thread. When draped on your tree these chains will look very gay.

PASTE

RUPERT and the BLUE

RUPERT HURRIES TO A SHOP

Now Guy Fawkes' Day is drawing nigh,
Some fireworks Rupert wants to buy.

But Mr. Hippo shakes his head,
" Sold out ! Why not have sweets instead ? "

IT is early November and Rupert is out on the common with Pong-Ping and the rabbit twins. " I say, look at that great pile of wood," says Reggie Rabbit. " What can be happening up there ? " " I know what it is," says Rupert. "It's the bonfire that Freddy and Ferdy Fox are building for the Fifth. They won't let anyone else join them—they want to have it all themselves. And that reminds me—I haven't bought any fireworks yet." " Nor have I," says Pong-Ping, " and there's not much time left. Let's go down to the village." They run down to Nutwood and into the shop, but Mr. Hippo shakes his head. " You're too late. Fireworks are all sold out," he says solemnly. " You should have come last week—I had plenty then." " Oh, what a pity," murmurs Pong-Ping. " That means we shan't have any to let off."

FIREWORK

RUPERT SEES PONG-PING'S FIND

Pong-Ping calls, " Rupert, come back here,
I've found a thing that's rather queer."

The friends look at the funny thing.
" It's not a cracker," says Pong-Ping.

The four friends are very disappointed as they come out of Mr. Hippo's shop. The rabbits walk away moodily, and Rupert is just about to follow them when Pong-Ping calls him back. " Just a minute, Rupert ! " he says. " Talking of fireworks, I picked up this queer thing this morning, look ! " Rummaging in his pocket he pulls out something blue, as thick as a pencil, with one end frayed and blackened. Rupert stares at it and frowns. " Surely it's a burned-out firework," he says. " It's one of those Chinese crackers, isn't it ? " " No," declares Pong-Ping. " I'm Chinese and I know all about Chinese crackers and this certainly isn't one. And it isn't a squib nor any kind of firework I've ever seen. I've an idea it is something far more mysterious." " But how exciting," says Rupert. " Where did you find it ? "

19

RUPERT WATCHES A BALLOON

" *I found it lying over there,"*
He waves his stick up in the air.

High in the sky floats a balloon,
They're sure it's going to land quite soon.

They pass great trees on either hand,
To find the spot where it will land.

Pong-Ping says, " Look what I have found."
And points to something on the ground.

Pong-Ping tells Rupert where he found the firework. " It was in the thick part of the wood not far from my house," he says. " Queer things sometimes happen in that wood, fizzing noises and rushing winds." " Oh, do let's go and look," says Rupert. Then he stops and stares at the sky. " Just look at that thing above the wood. It's a balloon and I do believe that's a real live man hanging underneath ! " The balloon hovers over the wood and then disappears behind the tops of the trees. " We really must find out what is happening," says Rupert. " That man on the balloon may be in trouble and need help, though how he got up there I can't imagine." They race downhill and into the wood. " There's no sign of him," says Pong-Ping, " but here are some more of those fireworks." He stoops to pick up two or three.

RUPERT LANDS IN A TREE

Then suddenly a windy shriek
Alarms both Rupert and the peke.

As quickly as it came it dies,
And both the pals begin to rise.

They must stop going up somehow,
So Rupert grabs a nearby bough.

" What did I tell you ! " Pong-Ping cries.
" I said you'd get a big surprise ! "

Rupert studies one of the blue fireworks. " It's very odd," he says. " I suppose this is just a firework, but why should anyone come into the middle of the wood to let it off ? " " Hush, listen," whispers his chum. " There's that fizzing noise I told you about." The sound increases to a low roar. It is followed by a furious gust of wind that gets warmer and warmer and the two friends find themselves lifted off their feet. Feeling himself floating upwards, Rupert clutches a small bough of a tree. Gradually the lifting ceases, and he finds he is able to sit among the branches. He calls out anxiously to Pong-Ping and a muffled voice tells him that his pal is safe in another tree, so he begins to clamber down very carefully. " I told you queer things were happening in this wood," says Pong-Ping, who is first to reach the ground.

RUPERT EXPLORES THE WOOD

Says Rupert, " Let us both explore."
But Pong-Ping won't play any more.

A strange man stands behind a tree,
He's watching Rupert secretly.

There, lying in a blackened ring,
He sees a most peculiar thing.

But then the stranger steps in sight,
And makes poor Rupert start in fright.

When he has got his breath back Rupert turns to his pal and with a grin says, " I'd like to know what caused the warm wind that sent us up into the air. Come on, let's try to find out." But Pong-Ping waves him off. " No fear, I've had enough," he declares. " I'm going home." So Rupert starts his search alone. He does not notice that a strange figure is watching him from behind a tree. " Hullo, there's something queer on the ground over there," he mutters. He hurries forward and discovers a ring of blackened grass. In the middle is a curious round object pierced with many small holes and with a knob on top. Rupert sees that a number of little blue fireworks are scattered near it. " This should be the secret," he cries, " but what is it ? " He turns sharply as the strange man suddenly comes forward.

RUPERT JOINS THE INVENTOR

" Hey, what d'you think you're doing there ? "
The strange man asks the little bear.

He growls, " Now just you come with me,
My new assistant you shall be."

" There, see my house ? " the stranger asks.
" I built it for some special tasks."

In every room are queer machines,
And Rupert wonders what it means.

" What might a little bear be doing here prying into my affairs ? " asks the stranger sternly. " Please," says Rupert, " we saw somebody hanging from a balloon and then we got caught in a sort of whirlwind and now I've found this. But I'll go away if you like." " No," grunts the man. " I have other plans for you." Picking up the round object he returns to where a black box is lying, picks it up too and marches Rupert firmly away. " I'm not going to hurt you, little bear," says the man, " but if you want me to explain what is happening you'll have to come and help. Look, there is my house. I built it specially for what I'm doing." In the hollow of the forest Rupert can see a curious square building. In a few minutes he is inside. The house is filled with a low buzzing sound and there are strange machines in every room.

RUPERT HEARS OF A NEW IDEA

The man tells Rupert, " Don't be long,
You need that food to make you strong."

" This work you'll help me with today,
Will quickly drive all fog away."

He says, " There's gas inside that ball.
It is so light it cannot fall."

Just as the man goes to the door,
The bear sees strange things on the floor.

The strange man gives Rupert some sandwiches and a glass of milk. "You will need to be strong for what you are going to do," he says. "It's November, and the fogs will be here soon. I've no time to lose. I don't like fogs so I'm making a wonderful thing called a Fog-lifter. Come on. I'll show you everything." And he leads him to an underground workshop. The man points to a large metal ball over his head. "That holds a powerful new lifting gas," he says. "It will lift fog or leaves or anything." "Is that what lifted Pong-Ping and me?" cries Rupert. "Very likely, if you got in its way," says the other. He turns away and Rupert pauses. "Look," he says. "Those round things are like the one I saw on the ground, and there are lots of blue fireworks stuck all around them."

RUPERT'S FRIEND GETS READY

The man says, " There's some gas in these,
And that should clear a fog with ease."

Then Rupert's told, " Now come with me,
How they explode next you shall see."

A fog comes up and fills the sky.
The new invention they can try!

" I wear thick woollies," says the man,
" I want to keep warm if I can."

The inventor comes back to Rupert's side. " The blue fireworks are the key to the whole idea," he says. " There's some of my new lifting gas pressed tight in each of them. When they go off they force it out in all directions. They are very powerful, and they make that strong wind you felt. Then it spreads, the gas goes up and takes all the fog with it. Follow me, and I'll finish explaining things." He leads the little bear up many steps. When they reach the top room the man stares at the windows. " Look up there," he cries. " It's fog, real fog. It must have come since we arrived. At last we can see if my invention really works." He puts on a muffler and a woolly cap, and then a fur jacket. " I don't like cold weather and I can't bear fog," he murmurs, " and where I'm going it's very cold indeed."

RUPERT HAS TO STAY BEHIND

Then on his back he puts a box.
And next, his belt he firmly locks.

He flings the front door open wide,
Then fog begins to swirl inside.

The man goes off and disappears,
And soon a buzzing Rupert hears.

It is the noise he's heard before.
It's followed by the wind once more.

The man goes down from the top room and chooses one of the round objects. Then he picks up a box which he fastens to his back. "Oh, please, what is that thing?" asks Rupert. "You had one like that when you found me in the wood." "No time to explain," says the man, opening the front door. "I must be off!" The fog swirls into the house but he steps straight out, and Rupert follows. "May I come with you?" calls the little bear. The man has nearly disappeared in the fog and his voice comes back faintly. "No, you might get lost if things don't go right. You'd better stay near the house." Rupert waits and listens and presently he hears the fizzing noise farther off than before. Gradually it swells to a roar, and again it is followed by a mighty wind. Next moment Rupert is blown right over.

RUPERT FEELS VERY SHAKEN

There's scarcely any fog to see,
The wind has cleared it easily.

The man has vanished now. But where?
To hunt for him goes Rupert Bear.

As Rupert looks up with a frown,
A great balloon comes floating down.

While Rupert dances round and round,
The man drops gently to the ground.

Rupert waits and trembles, wondering if he is to be carried up into the air as before, and he clutches a tuft of grass. To his relief he is lifted only a few inches and then drops back. The air below has become quite clear so that he can see right into the wood. "Well, the invention has worked," he thinks, "but the man has disappeared. Where can he have gone so quickly?" The little bear glances upwards to

find that the fog is now a long way above the trees. As he looks a dim shape appears through the mist. In another moment it is clear and he can see that it is another balloon dropping gently, and hanging from it is the figure of the inventor. Rupert runs forward in great excitement to meet him. "Oo, this is thrilling!" he shouts. "How did you make that thing on your back turn into a balloon?"

RUPERT SEES THE FOG-LIFTER

"The fog has cleared for half a mile,"
The man tells Rupert with a smile.

He makes them both a cup of tea,
As Rupert questions eagerly.

"This one is bigger than the rest,"
He says, " and you shall do the test."

So Rupert looks at all his kit,
And hopes that he can manage it.

When the inventor is safely down, he smiles at Rupert. " That's the first time I've been able to try my fog-lifter on real fog and it works perfectly. All the fog has gone for half a mile round my house. Now come in again. I want to warm myself." They hurry indoors and the man draws off some boiling water from one of his machines to make some tea. " You said you wanted me to help you," Rupert reminds him. The inventor takes Rupert into another room. " I'm tired of making so many trials of my new invention," he says. " My latest fog-lifter is the strongest yet, and I want you to set it off." He points to a round contraption larger than the others and filled with bigger blue fireworks. Then he gets another box for Rupert to strap on his back and finally he goes to find a fur coat.

RUPERT PREPARES FOR THE TEST

He tells the man he won't be cold,
Then listens to the things he's told.

They set off for a distant glade,
Poor Rupert feels a bit afraid.

" Just press that knob there with your toe,"
The bear is told, " then up you'll go."

The old inventor runs away,
But Rupert knows that he must stay.

Rupert looks at the preparations the inventor is making. " I don't need a fur coat," he laughs. " I don't mind the cold." So the man straps the box firmly to his back. Fixed to the box is a curly piece of wire ending in a button which he puts in Rupert's left hand. " This is my safety box," he says. " There's some of my new lifting gas in it." Then, carrying the latest fog-lifter in a cloth, he leads Rupert out. At last they reach a place where the fog is still quite thick. There the man puts the fog-lifter on the ground. " Now, all you have to do is stand on it," he says. " When I am safely out of the way you must put your foot on that knob in the middle and push firmly. When you go up with the fog, press the button in your left hand, and you will come down very gently." With that he hurries away.

RUPERT FALLS FROM THE SKY

Then Rupert stands in readiness,
He gives the knob a swift, sharp press.

There comes a crackling and a roar,
And Rupert's in the air once more.

The bear floats up and up with ease,
Until he's right above the trees.

The great balloon begins to swell.
" So far," thinks Rupert, " all's gone well."

Rupert waits until he can no longer hear the inventor's footsteps, then he plucks up enough courage to tread firmly on the knob of the round object beneath him. At once there is a crackling noise and, with a loud hiss that swells to a roar, all the blue fireworks catch light together, forcing the lifting gas out in a wide circle. Rupert is very frightened. The air becomes warm, and he finds himself carried very swiftly up through the trees. Before he can recover his wits Rupert is well above the forest with nothing to hold on to. " This is awful ! " he gasps. Then he remembers the inventor's words, and presses the button in his left hand. A balloon swells from the box on his back and as it fills out to its full size, Rupert glances over his shoulder and catches a glimpse of it. " Whew, it's worked ! " he breathes.

Rupert and the Blue Firework

RUPERT'S CHUMS RUN TO HELP

But Rupert just floats round and round,
He cannot seem to reach the ground.

Upon the hill, Rex Rabbit cries,
" Can that be Rupert in the skies? "

The pals don't know what it's about,
All they can hear is Rupert's shout.

Says Pong-Ping, " I know what to do !
Bring Edward Trunk back here, you two."

Rupert expects to drop gently to the ground as the inventor has said, but though he waits nothing seems to happen. He floats along at the same height, drifting over the tree-tops. Meanwhile Pong-Ping has run out of his house to find out why the fog has suddenly disappeared. On the common he meets Rex and Reggie Rabbit. "I say, look up there !" gasps Rex. "There's someone hanging from a balloon. It's just like Rupert." "It *is* Rupert !" says Pong-Ping. Spying his pals on the common below him, Rupert calls out and tries to explain what has happened. "I'm not heavy enough to bring the balloon down !" he shouts. Pong-Ping stares. "I can't make out what he's talking about, but Rupert's in trouble," he says. "I'll get some rope from my house while you two run and find Edward Trunk."

RUPERT HOVERS OVERHEAD

Pong-Ping has come back with a rope.
He calls, "This is our only hope."

"This rope to Rupert we must throw,"
Says Pong-Ping, "when he passes low."

The bear comes close enough at length,
And Edward throws with all his strength.

Alas, the first throw falls too short.
He throws again. Hooray, it's caught!

The two rabbits return with Edward just as the little peke arrives with a long coil of rope. " Well, what do you want with me ? And what is Rupert doing floating in the sky ? " demands Edward. Pong-Ping leads them uphill. " I saw that Rupert was drifting towards the highest part of the common," he puffs. " He won't be far above us when he gets here, so I thought we might throw a rope. I sent for you because you can throw the farthest." When he hears Pong-Ping's idea Edward agrees readily. The light wind blows Rupert gently towards the hill-top, and his pals shout to tell him what they are going to do. Then Edward flings the rope high in the air. To everyone's dismay it misses and falls to the ground. Edward coils it in haste and throws again. This time his aim is straight and Rupert grabs the rope.

RUPERT REACHES THE GROUND

Upon the rope the bear holds tight,
While Edward pulls with all his might.

With Reggie holding Rupert's hands,
Pong-Ping unstraps him as he lands.

"There's Mr. Bear," calls out the peke.
"He isn't near enough to speak."

They tie the rope around a tree,
It's safe as far as they can see.

Rupert grips the rope very firmly while Edward pulls him out of the sky. When he is nearly down, Reggie runs forward and grabs his arms to hold him there, and Pong-Ping hurries to tie the rope to the balloon. "Whew, that *was* a queer adventure," says Rupert in relief. "The inventor forgot that I wasn't heavy enough to bring the balloon down." Then he tells them all that has happened. "I wonder what we'd better do now," Rupert murmurs. "This thing belongs to the inventor. I wish I knew how to let the lifting gas out of the balloon. If we let go of it, it will shoot up again." As they go towards the wood there is a shout from Pong-Ping. "I can see your daddy over there, Rupert," he calls. "Oo, I'd like to show him this thing," says Rupert. So they tie the balloon to a strong old tree stump.

RUPERT RETURNS WITH MR. BEAR

To Mr. Bear the chums all run,
And Rupert tells him what they've done.

But Father thinks the man was wrong,
To keep the little bear so long.

Back to the forest glade they trot,
With Mr. Bear to see the spot.

When they arrive, to their dismay,
They find the things have gone away.

From the hill-top the little pals catch sight of Mr. Bear in the distance. They run to join him and he turns in surprise. " What's been happening ? " he asks. " The fog disappeared quite suddenly and then I saw a balloon in the sky, but that has disappeared, too." " Yes, and I was with it," laughs Rupert and then he tells his daddy the whole story. Mr. Bear scratches his head. " The man shouldn't have sent you up like that," he says. The little bear begs him to look at the balloon which he has left tied to the tree stump. So they hurry to the spot, but both the balloon and the black box have disappeared. " Are you sure it hasn't broken away and sailed up in the sky ? " asks Mr. Bear. " No, no," declares Rupert. " That can't have happened. See, there is Pong-Ping's rope that fastened it. Someone has coiled it up."

RUPERT SURPRISES HIS MUMMY

But as they all prepare to go,
Pong-Ping calls, "Someone's here, I know."

" Why there's the man," cries Rupert Bear.
" I recognise him by his hair."

" The next strange wind won't frighten me,"
Says Pong-Ping, and the rest agree.

Says Rupert, " I wish you had seen
The old inventor's fog machine !"

The pals are strolling away when Pong-Ping, who has paused to pick up his rope, calls out, " There's someone moving about in the wood ! " Rupert and Mr. Bear return to see a hurrying figure. " Why, it's the inventor ! " says Rupert. " He must have watched us all the time and when we ran off to fetch Daddy, he untied the balloon. He knew how to let the lifting gas out of it and, look, there is the square box under his arm ! " " I'm glad to have seen that funny man," laughs Pong-Ping. " When those sudden winds come I shall know he is only practising his fog-lifters." When Rupert gets home and tells the whole queer story to Mrs. Bear, she shakes her head and says, " You might have floated away with the balloon. If that man dislikes fog it would be safer for him to take a drop of my home-made syrup ! "

HOW TO MAKE A BIRD-TABLE

FIX NAIL THROUGH CENTRE OF BIRD-TABLE

PLACE POINT OF NAIL ON FLAT END OF BROOM HANDLE OR STAKE. HAMMER NAIL FIRMLY INTO WOOD

ANOTHER WAY OF MAKING A TABLE-TOP USING NARROW STRIPS OF WOOD

WOODEN BARS NAILED ACROSS UNDERSIDE OF TABLE

LENGTH OF OLD BROOM HANDLE

STAKE CUT FROM TREE BRANCH

THE THINGS YOU NEED
A piece of wood about 15 inches square for table-top.
A piece of broom handle or garden stake about 2 feet long.
A hammer and a stout nail.

SHARPEN THIS END

MR. BEAR has helped Rupert to make a bird-table for the garden. The little bear watches from the window and sees the birds flutter down to peck at the crumbs he has left for them. Near the bird-table is a dish filled with water where the birds can refresh themselves. The bird-table is easy to make and the black panel on this page shows you how it is done. The table-top can be either a single piece of wood or several narrow strips. Drive the pointed end of the stick into the ground by hammering the centre of the table-top. Now sprinkle crumbs on the table and you will soon have some pretty little visitors. Perhaps you will recognise some of them in the set of cards from Rupert's nature album.

RUPERT'S FEATHERED FRIENDS

BLUE-TIT

LINNET

MAGPIE

STARLING

KINGFISHER

SONG-THRUSH

ROBIN

TREE-SPARROW

SWALLOW

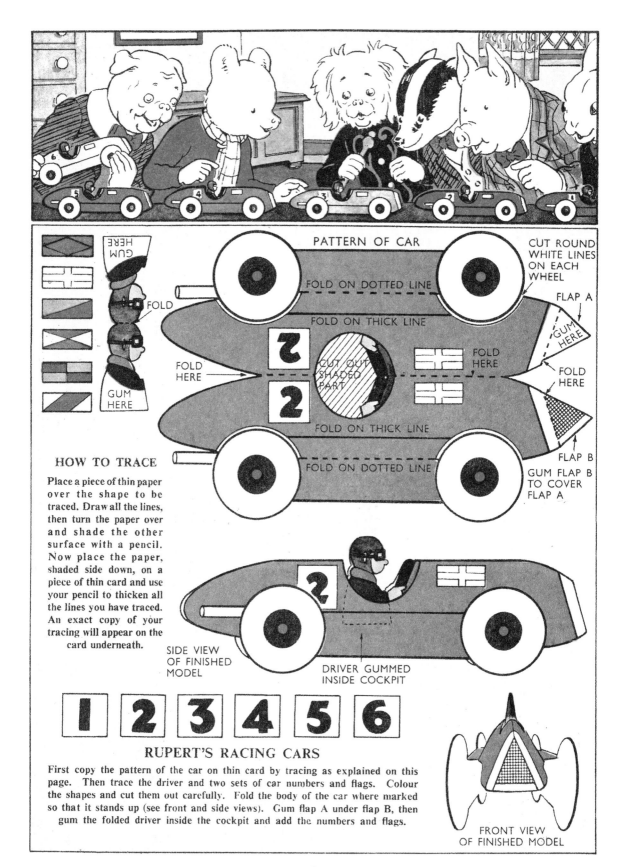

PATTERN OF CAR

GUM HERE

FOLD

GUM HERE

CUT ROUND WHITE LINES ON EACH WHEEL

FOLD ON DOTTED LINE

FOLD ON THICK LINE

FLAP A

GUM HERE

FOLD HERE

FOLD HERE

FOLD HERE

CUT OUT SHADED PART

FOLD ON THICK LINE

FLAP B

GUM FLAP B TO COVER FLAP A

FOLD ON DOTTED LINE

HOW TO TRACE

Place a piece of thin paper over the shape to be traced. Draw all the lines, then turn the paper over and shade the other surface with a pencil. Now place the paper, shaded side down, on a piece of thin card and use your pencil to thicken all the lines you have traced. An exact copy of your tracing will appear on the card underneath.

SIDE VIEW OF FINISHED MODEL

DRIVER GUMMED INSIDE COCKPIT

1 2 3 4 5 6

RUPERT'S RACING CARS

First copy the pattern of the car on thin card by tracing as explained on this page. Then trace the driver and two sets of car numbers and flags. Colour the shapes and cut them out carefully. Fold the body of the car where marked so that it stands up (see front and side views). Gum flap A under flap B, then gum the folded driver inside the cockpit and add the numbers and flags.

FRONT VIEW OF FINISHED MODEL

MAKE A HOLE
IN EACH PIECE
TO TAKE
KNOTTED STRING

RUPERT'S WORD FAN

The word fan has six pieces of thin card each bearing a letter of the word RUPERT. In the large fan shown above the shape containing the letter U is your pattern. Trace the shape on thin card, as described on the facing page, and put in the letter U. Cut out this shape and, placing it on a piece of card, draw round it to make a further five outlines. Now make separate tracings of the remaining five large letters and add one to each shape. Colour the shapes and cut them out, making a hole in the centre circle of each, then thread them on string, which should be knotted closely at the back and front to keep the pieces together. Now shuffle letters about and see how many words you can make.

RUPERT and the AUTUMN

RUPERT HEARS FERDY'S NEWS

As Rupert rests beneath a tree,
He thinks, " What can that music be ? "

Says Ferdy Fox, " Why, it's a fair !
Do come with me—I'm going there ! "

THE day is warm, and Rupert, who has been for a walk by himself, is resting at the foot of a tree when a distant sound of music reaches his ears. He sits up and listens. " Where can that be coming from ? " he murmurs with a frown. " And what is it ? It doesn't sound quite like a band." At that moment he happens to notice a small figure running across the brow of the hill. " Surely that's one of the Fox brothers," says Rupert, scrambling to his feet. " Yes, it is Ferdy ! I must ask him what has happened." He gives chase and soon catches the little fox. " Hullo, are you coming too ? " asks Ferdy breathlessly. " Look, there's a fair just opened up at Robin Down. I'm on my way to see it." " Ooo ! I love fairs ! " exclaims Rupert, falling in step with Ferdy. " Let's go along together ! "

PRIMROSE

RUPERT FEELS RATHER GLUM

Sighs Edward, " I've no money here,
I can't go to the fair. Oh dear !"

While Rupert's saying, " Never mind—"
He has a most surprising find !

As Rupert and Ferdy reach the fair they meet Edward Trunk, who is gazing longingly at the gaily coloured tents and side-shows. " Hullo, Edward, you're looking very glum," says the little bear. " Aren't you going inside ? " " I've been inside, and there are lots of lovely things in there," says Edward with a heavy sigh. " There are racers and roundabouts and coconut shies and skittles and a helter-skelter, but they all cost money and I've spent all my pocket money. I haven't got a penny." " Nor have I," says Rupert. " Oh dear, neither have I," sighs Ferdy. The chums ponder for a moment, then Edward says, " Perhaps we'd better go home and ask for some money first." Rather sadly they turn away, but before they have gone far Rupert catches sight of a dark object partly hidden in a patch of long grass.

RUPERT RETURNS A PURSE

"Some money!" Ferdy shouts. "Let's go!"
But Rupert stops and murmurs, "No!"

"Let's ask that man! I'll run and see
If he has dropped it carelessly."

The man turns round at Rupert's call—
"Have you lost anything at all?"

The man says, "Well, I do declare!
You are an honest little bear!"

Rupert picks up the thing he has seen in the grass. "Why, it's a purse!" he exclaims. "And it sounds as if there's money in it. We must find out whose it is." Edward nods his head. "We can't keep it," he says. But Ferdy gets angry. "You sillies," he grumbles, as he stalks away. "We could have spent it at the fair." Rupert wonders what to do. "Let's see if this purse belongs to those people," he says,

pointing. The pals soon catch up with the people. "Have you lost anything?" asks Rupert. The gentleman feels in his pocket and says, "My purse has gone! I must have dropped it back there." "Then here it is," says Rupert. "I'm glad we've found the owner." "Well, you are an honest little bear," laughs the man as he lifts him up. "How would you both like to come to the fair with us?"

RUPERT ENJOYS THE FAIR

And in return he pays for three ;
The chums try everything with glee.

" Now here's a shilling—it`s for you,
And here is one for Edward, too."

" A shilling each to spend ! Hooray !
We really are in luck today ! "

" Throw first, then, Rupert," Edward cries,
" And do your best to win a prize ! "

Rupert and Edward are thrilled at going to the fair with their new friends, and the gentleman pays for everything. At last they stop for buns and ices, and the gentleman smiles. " It's time for us to go now," he says, " but you can stay for a while if you like, so here's a shilling for each of you to have some more fun by yourselves." And next minute the two pals are alone. " Aren't we lucky ! I hardly know where to start," laughs Rupert. Edward thinks solemnly. " I'm a strong thrower," he decides. " I'd like to try the skittles once more." " Right-ho, let's do them first," agrees Rupert, and they go up to the gipsy woman in charge of the sideshow. " There's a special prize if you can knock down the two black skittles without upsetting the rest of them," she says. " Good, and Rupert can try first," says Edward.

RUPERT WINS A QUAINT PRIZE

*"The black one! What a lucky throw!
I didn't really aim, you know."*

*The gipsy lady nods her head,
"I thought you'd miss—you've won instead!"*

*"Look, this is what I've got for you,
A lovely jug—I've only two."*

*"Throw hard!" says Rupert Bear. "Oh my!
It looks as though you've thrown too high."*

Rupert wants to win the special prize, so he stands very steady and then throws the ball. "Oh, grand shot, you've knocked down one of the black skittles!" cries Edward. "That was just luck," laughs Rupert. "I was aiming at the other one!" The second ball flies wide, but the third ball goes very straight—and down falls the other black skittle. "Fancy that!" gasps the gipsy woman. "No one else has done that the whole of the week!" The gipsy points to a large china jug. "There is your prize," she says. "You can use it for holding flowers. I didn't think many people would win them so I only got two of the jugs." "Then I'm going to win the other one," says Edward. He hurls his first ball with great force, but it hits the canvas where it is worn and goes right through. A shout comes from the other side.

RUPERT IS GIVEN A PROMISE

Asks Edward, " Did you hear that shout?
I wonder what it's all about."

" I'd like to know who spoilt my hat,"
The man says crossly. " Look at that!"

When Edward tells what he has done,
The gipsy laughs, and thinks it's fun.

"The other jug is for your friend,
If you're successful in the end."

The angry voice goes on and when the pals peep behind the stall they see the ringmaster and a clown. The tall man looks very annoyed. " Just wait until I find who dented my hat ! " he storms. " Oh, golly, it must have been my shot that knocked his hat off, Rupert," whispers Edward. " What can I do about it ? " He backs quietly out of sight and the two pals gaze at each other in dismay. When they tell the gipsy woman what has happened she gives a chuckle. " That's the funniest thing I've heard this month ! " she says. " Well, that poor man didn't seem to think it was funny," says Rupert. The woman still smiles. " Don't worry," she says. " I'll tell him it was an accident. Meanwhile, take your prize jug and if you can bring it back full of primroses I'll give your friend the other jug in reward for making me laugh."

RUPERT TAKES HIS JUG HOME

With envy both the foxes stand
And stare at Rupert's jug so grand.

" What, primroses? You silly thing !
They only flower in the spring."

The foxes scoff at Rupert Bear,
Then scamper off to see the fair.

As Rupert hurries on his way,
He thinks, " What will my Mummy say ? "

As Rupert and Edward hurry away from Robin Down they meet Ferdy with his brother Freddy. "So you *did* keep that purse," cries Ferdy, "and you've been having a good time at the fair with the money in it." "You're quite wrong," says Rupert, and he tells them the story of the jug. "The gipsy woman said that if I took it back full of primroses she'd give us another," he says. "Yah," jeers Ferdy, "there are no primroses in autumn !" Although the two foxes are so jealous, Rupert feels he would like to share the good fortune. "That kind gentleman gave us a shilling each," he says. "Edward paid for the skittles, but mine hasn't been touched. Would you like to take it and spend it at the fair?" The foxes take the money and scamper away, while Rupert and Edward separate and go home.

RUPERT MEETS THE SCOTTIE

" I won this jug all by myself,
Let's keep it for the mantel-shelf ! "

" Now, who is that ? " says Rupert. " Why !
It's Jock the Scottie running by."

So Rupert calls, " Come here, old boy ! "
And Jock the puppy jumps for joy.

" Whatever can this primrose mean ?
And where has Philip's puppy been ? "

Inside the cottage Mrs. Bear stares at Rupert's prize. " I've never seen anything quite like that ! " she gasps. " Isn't it lovely," says the little bear eagerly. " The gipsy lady said if I brought it back with primroses in it she would give the other one to Edward." " What ! Primroses in autumn ? " smiles his mother. But Rupert has already started out. On the common a little black dog passes him. " Hullo " he thinks. " There's Jock the Scottie." Rupert calls to Jock and the little dog runs up to him. " Where have you been ? And why isn't your master Philip with you ? " he asks. " And what is that on your back ? " He picks a small yellow flower out of the fur. Jock goes on his way, but Rupert stands gazing at what he has found. " It's a real primrose ! " he gasps. " So Ferdy was wrong. There *are* autumn primroses."

RUPERT CALLS ON PHILIP

" Since Jock's the only one who knows,
I'll follow him—look, there he goes ! "

" It's no use asking me, I fear !
I'm sure he didn't find it here ! "

Then Philip takes his little friend
To search the garden end to end.

" Look, Mummy ! Here's a primrose—see ?
Which Jock the doggie found for me ! "

Rupert decides quickly. " If I'm to fill that jug I must find where Jock got this primrose," he thinks. " I expect he was rolling in a bed of them. But where ? " Following the dog, he sees him disappear inside the gate of Philip's house. The boy is in the garden and Rupert runs up to him. " I say, look what I've found on your Scottie's back," he cries. " It's a primrose," says Philip, mystified. " How

strange ! They are spring flowers." He is as puzzled as Rupert. " I've no idea where he found that primrose," he says, " There are certainly none in this garden, as you can see." Rupert thanks him and hurries back to his own cottage. " Mummy, look," he cries. " Here is one primrose. Please put it in water while I try to get some more. I must try to fill that jug with them before the fair closes tomorrow."

RUPERT VISITS THE PROFESSOR

Soon Rupert stands where first he met
Young Jock, the little Scottie pet.

" The old Professor I will ask,
Perhaps he'll help me with my task."

" Your clever master's sure to know
Exactly where the flowers grow."

" An autumn primrose ? Well, that's queer !
I've never seen such flowers here ! "

Leaving his mother looking very puzzled, Rupert runs back to the spot on the common where he met Jock. " The little dog was coming from the direction of that wood," he murmurs. Then he gets an idea. " The old Professor's house is near the edge of the wood," he thinks. " I'll go and ask him if he has been growing primroses lately." He hurries over the hill until he spies the Professor's dwarf servant at work.

He listens in surprise to Rupert's story. " I've been working in this garden all my life," he says, " but I've never yet seen an autumn primrose, and yet you say you've got one ! You'd better tell my master." They find the Professor resting near his greenhouses. " You do bring me the oddest question, little bear," he sighs on hearing about the mystery. " This time I'm afraid I can't help you."

RUPERT STARTS HIS SEARCH

" Ah well," says Rupert with a sigh,
" It's time that I went home—goodbye ! "

At bedtime Rupert plans to look
Much farther for that primrose nook.

His mummy, standing at the gate,
Says, " Now dear, don't get home too late."

" Ah, there goes Jock ! He's on his way
To roam the wood again today ! "

The old Professor makes Rupert promise that if he does find any autumn primroses he will bring him some. " My garden contains most things, but those would be new to me," he smiles. Then the little bear decides that it is too late to search farther, so he goes home. As he is climbing into bed he gets another idea. " I say, mummy," he calls, " tomorrow is my last chance of finding any primroses, so may I spend the whole day exploring those woods ? " " Perhaps ! " laughs his mummy. The next day is bright and sunny, so Mrs. Bear gives way to Rupert's wish and he sets out with a bag of food to last him all day. He makes straight for the thick woodland, but finds it so gloomy that he does not like to go in alone. Then he sees Jock moving across the common. " He's heading for the wood," he whispers.

RUPERT REACHES A GARDEN

Then Rupert, on his hands and knees,
Starts scrambling underneath the trees.

" Why, here's a hole right through the wall !
I can't get through—it's much too small."

" I'll climb the wall—it won't take long,
Because the ivy's very strong."

So up he climbs, and doesn't stop
Until he gets right to the top.

Rupert goes in pursuit. "He seems to know the way quite well," he mutters. Jock trots steadily forward, and at length disappears amongst dense bushes. The little bear burrows his way through, and on the other side he is faced with a stone wall. There is no sign of the dog, but Rupert notices that one of the lowest stones has started to crumble, leaving a small gap near the ground. "That's all right for Jock," he thinks as he examines the hole, "but it's too small for me." Then he notices that the stonework is partly covered with thick ivy. "I could climb that easily," he murmurs. "I wonder if it would matter." Using a piece of string from his pocket, he hangs the paper bag from his shoulder and then clambers up the ivy branches. In a few minutes Rupert is peering down into a beautiful garden.

RUPERT FINDS THE PRIMROSES

And when he starts to look around,
He sees Jock rolling on the ground.

"This is a most amazing thing !
The garden looks as if it's spring !"

"I hope you won't be cross with me,
I came here after Jock, you see !"

"I can't quite recognise you yet,
But surely you and I have met ?"

At first Rupert can see nothing of Jock. Moving along the top of the wall the little bear finds another ivy plant growing up the other side and he climbs down it into the garden. There he finds the Scottie rolling contentedly in a flower bed. "They are primroses," gasps Rupert, "real primroses ! What sort of garden is this ? There are all sorts of spring flowers growing here as well as autumn ones !" Jock wags his tail at Rupert and then he suddenly turns and runs away at the sound of footsteps. Next moment a little girl appears. "Oh, dear," says Rupert nervously. "I know I oughtn't to be here, but I was following Jock the Scottie." He pauses and looks at her. "I say," he adds, "surely you are Mary-Quite-Contrary ?" "Yes, I am," says the little girl, "and no wonder I'm contrary. Just look at my garden !"

RUPERT'S FRIEND IS WORRIED

" My garden's all gone wrong, somehow,
The flowers of spring are blooming now ! "

Says Mary, " Here's my grandpapa !
Let's go and tell him who you are ! "

" Though he's a friend of yours, my dear,
I don't know what he's doing here ! "

" May I look round the place with you ?
And then, perhaps, I'll find a clue."

Rupert stares at the little girl. " I think your garden is wonderful," he says. " People told me that I couldn't find primroses in autumn, but you've got some lovely beds of them." " That's what I mean," cries Mary. " The spring flowers keep coming out all through the year and I'm afraid they'll die. I don't want to lose them." She stops suddenly as a stately old gentleman approaches slowly. " This is my grandfather," says Mary as she introduces Rupert, who then has a chance to tell his story and explain why he came. " So you want primroses, do you ? " says the old man. " Well, there are plenty here, but it's worrying us to see them in the autumn. Somebody is playing tricks with my garden, but who it is I can't imagine." " This is exciting ! " cries Rupert. " May I see if I can find any clues ? "

RUPERT KEEPS A LOOK-OUT

They find, as they are walking round,
A little tunnel near the ground.

" I wonder if Jock's been here, too,"
Says Rupert, as he scrambles through.

" I'll eat my lunch up in the tree,
This branch is just the height for me."

He sees a figure disappear,
And gasps, " Now that is very queer ! "

The old gentleman tells Rupert he is free to explore, so Mary shows him round the garden. Soon they reach a part where the grass is very high. " What is this small tunnel through the grass ? " murmurs Rupert. " Jock must have come this way, too." He pushes his way through, but Mary hangs back. " I must go and join grandpa," she says. " Be sure and let us know if you find anything interesting." Beyond the high grass Rupert finds a very rough patch of garden with many weeds. " There are no clues here," he thinks, " so I'll have my lunch and decide what to do next." He climbs on to a branch of a tree, and is soon enjoying his sandwiches. Presently he sees a tiny figure skim through the undergrowth and disappear. " It looked like an imp," he gasps. He scrambles down and gives chase along a faint footpath.

RUPERT CHASES AN IMP

*Then Rupert follows, shouting " Hey !
Come back ! You needn't run away ! "*

*Sighs Rupert, " Well, I cannot see
Where he has gone ! Where can he be ? "*

*And just as he gives up the chase,
He meets a big elf, face to face.*

*" An Imp of Spring is up to pranks.
He certainly deserves no thanks ! "*

Thrusting his way through some thick bushes, Rupert is in time to see the imp disappear once more. "He knows I'm following," mutters Rupert. "Why is he running away from me?" Still keeping to the little path, he finds that it leads straight to an old sundial, and there it stops. "Well, this *is* queer," he says. "Did he come all this way just to see the time?" Rupert is about to turn back, when he comes face to face with a much larger imp. "You're one of the Autumn Elves, aren't you?" he exclaims. "What is going on in this garden?" "You may well ask!" says the elf angrily. "Here we are, trying to do our proper work and make the garden right for autumn, while all the time one of the Imps of Spring has got loose, and is filling it with spring flowers, and is overworking the plants."

RUPERT HURRIES TO THE HOUSE

The Imp's track finishes nearby
A sundial—Rupert wonders why.

Then Rupert thinks. " Now, first," says he,
" Come back to Mary's house with me."

And Rupert waves and gives a shout,
Just as the other two come out.

Cries Rupert, " Why, where is the elf?
I brought him here just now, myself !"

" So that's what is happening," cries Rupert. " The imp ran straight to this sundial—then he seemed to vanish." " Yes," says the elf. " I've wondered why this little track finished at the sundial." " Well, I'll help you to try to find out," replies Rupert. " But first I wish you'd come and explain to Mary and her grandfather." And he leads the way back through the tall grass. Rupert reaches the house just as Mary and her grandfather walk out. " I've solved the whole thing," cries the little bear. " One of the Imps of Spring is still at work, and one of the Autumn Elves is after him. When he catches him all will be well." " Imps and elves?" says the old gentleman. " There aren't such things." " But there are ! " insists Rupert. " There's one here, look." He turns round, but the Autumn Elf is nowhere to be seen.

RUPERT PUZZLES THE OLD MAN

" I saw a little track just here,
Let's follow it—it's very clear."

Though Rupert begs the elf to stay,
He's scared and quickly runs away.

" Here's where I saw the Imp of Spring,
But now I can't see anything."

"The elf has gone—I wonder where.
He can't be far," says Rupert Bear.

The old gentleman looks hard at Rupert. "Are you serious about this fairy tale?" he asks. "But it *isn't* a fairy tale," insists the little bear. "Do please come and let me show you the small footpath." He leads the way, and just beyond the tall grass he spies the Autumn Elf. "Why did you leave me?" asks Rupert. "Hi, who are you talking to?" calls Mary from behind. At the sound of her voice the elf leaps away out of sight. Rupert again tries to explain, but as the others cannot understand, he leads them along the track to the sundial. "It's many years since I've been to this spot," murmurs the old gentleman. "I'd almost forgotten it. How odd that the track leads here and no farther." They walk round it thoughtfully, but Rupert quietly slips away. "Why does that elf keep disappearing?" he thinks.

RUPERT TELLS THE GOOD NEWS

The elf says, " We feel very shy
When any grown-up folks come by."

" Now to the sundial let us go,
And I will tell you all I know."

Then Mary's grandpa calls the friends.
He's standing where the imp's trail ends.

" Someone has moved the sundial's arm,
And that is what has done the harm."

Suddenly Rupert is startled by a loud whisper. " P-s-s-t, have you found anything else ? " says the voice. Turning sharply, he sees the Autumn Elf hiding in a small tree. " Why do you keep on running away ? " Rupert asks. " We never show ourselves to grown-ups if we can help it," says the elf, " but if . . . " Suddenly he breaks off and leaps away once again. Next moment Mary appears at Rupert's side. " I say, I saw whom you were talking to that time ! " she cries. " Did I frighten him away ? " Before Rupert can answer Mary's question there is a loud call from the old gentleman, and the two little people run to join him. " You're searching for clues," says the old man. " Well, do you see anything queer about this sundial ? The arm is pointing at the sun. While it's in that position it could never tell the time at all ! "

RUPERT IS LEFT BEHIND

He tries to put the sundial right,
And then the imp leaps into sight.

" Oh look ! " cries Rupert, " there they are !
I can't catch up--they've gone too far."

The friendly elf says, " It's no good !
He's got away—I knew he would."

They hear what Rupert has to tell,
And think he's done extremely well.

The old gentleman tries to correct the arm of the sundial. " Hullo, it's loose," he says, " and so is the plate underneath." As he lifts it up, revealing a hole right down through the stonework, a tiny figure shoots out. " It's the Imp of Spring," shouts Rupert. The Autumn Elf has been watching, and in a flash he leaps in pursuit. In great excitement Rupert runs after them. The imp and the elf dodge so fast through the rough grass that Rupert loses sight of them until he finds the Autumn Elf standing alone on a branch. " That imp has got away this time," laughs the tiny creature, " but don't worry, we'll catch him and send him home. Then the garden will grow the right flowers." Rupert returns to tell the others. " This is wonderful," says the old man. " You have solved the mystery of the garden."

RUPERT PICKS THE FLOWERS

" Let's point the arm the proper way,
And put the sundial right," they say.

Says Mary, " I'll run on ahead,
And lead you to the primrose bed."

" These flowers are what you came here for,"
Laughs Mary, " look, I've picked some more!"

Then Rupert Bear is homeward bound,
With all the flowers he has found.

Mary's grandfather shakes his head. " I should never have believed there really were any imps and elves unless I'd seen them," he murmurs. " I must be more careful what I say in future." He looks at his watch, and then he puts the arm of the sundial back so that it tells the right time. " And now, please may I have some of the primroses ? " asks Rupert. " Why, of course," cries Mary, and she leads the way back towards her flower-beds. Then she fetches a nice little basket. " Now that the garden has been put right I hope that I shan't be contrary any more," she laughs. " It has all been your doing, so you may keep the basket as a reward, and you shall have all the primroses. The plants will be better without them." When the basket is filled right to the top, her grandfather joins them, and they bid farewell to Rupert.

RUPERT SURPRISES HIS CHUM

As Rupert hurries through the wood,
He says, " There's Edward Trunk ! Oh, good ! "

" You've found some primroses, I see !
They look like magic flowers to me ! "

" We'll have to hurry to the fair,
We haven't any time to spare ! "

Says Mrs. Bear, " How very queer !
Where did you find these flowers, dear ? "

Rupert makes his way through the wood and into the open country. " Good, now I know where I am," he thinks. The first person he meets is Edward Trunk. " Hullo, Rupert," says Edward, " I've had no luck. I've searched all day without finding a single primrose." " Just look at what I've got in this basket ! " laughs the little bear. " They're real primroses," gasps Edward. He can hardly wait to hear how

Rupert succeeded in his search. " We haven't much time to spare," he says. " We must hurry if we are to get to the fair before it closes." So the two little pals race over the common towards Rupert's home. Inside the cottage Mrs. Bear listens to the story of how the primroses were found. " You can have the basket, mummy," says Rupert. " And we'll put the primroses in the prize jug."

RUPERT CLAIMS THE JUG

The pockets of the jug are filled,
And Rupert and his chum are thrilled.

So off the friends run, very fast,
And reach the gipsy's tent, at last.

The gipsy says, " I'm glad you've come.
The other jug is for your chum."

The foxes stand and stare. " Oh why
Do you have all the luck ? " they cry.

Mrs. Bear fetches the jug, and they fill the side pockets full of primroses. "Hooray," cries Rupert. "There will be enough over to make a bunch for mummy and a bunch for the old professor." Then he and Edward set off again with the jug and one spare bunch, and hurry to Robin Down. They reach the fair just as it is beginning to close. A minute later they find the gipsy and show her the jug and its precious contents. She gazes at the primroses she has taken from the jug. "What lovely flowers !" she exclaims. "'I can't imagine how you found them in the autumn, little bear, but I haven't forgotten the promise I made to you. Your friend shall have the jug !" Edward takes it and thanks her joyfully. Then they say goodbye and leave the fair. On their way they meet the Fox brothers and tell them the story.

RUPERT FINISHES HIS TASK

" It's getting late, and as you know,
I still have somewhere else to go."

Then up runs Rupert, panting, " Please,
I've brought some flowers—look at these ! "

" Are these for me ?   How very kind.
But, Rupert, what strange things you find ! "

So Rupert's pleased—now he can tell
How everything has turned out well !

"Are there any primroses left in Mary's garden ? Could we get some ?" asks Ferdy. "No, this is the last bunch," says Rupert. "You can have one primrose each and the rest are for the old professor." Then Edward says, "I must hurry now and show my prize to everybody at home." So he lumbers away happily, and Rupert makes off to find the professor. The story of the primroses astounds

Rupert's wise friend. "Fancy that !" he says. "The Imps of Spring don't come to my garden." "I'm sure they do," laughs Rupert, "only you never see them. It's lucky for you that none of them tries to work in the autumn or you'd be worried just as Mary was." Then he takes his prize home and tells the full tale of his adventure. "Well, that Autumn Elf should be grateful to you," says Mrs. Bear.

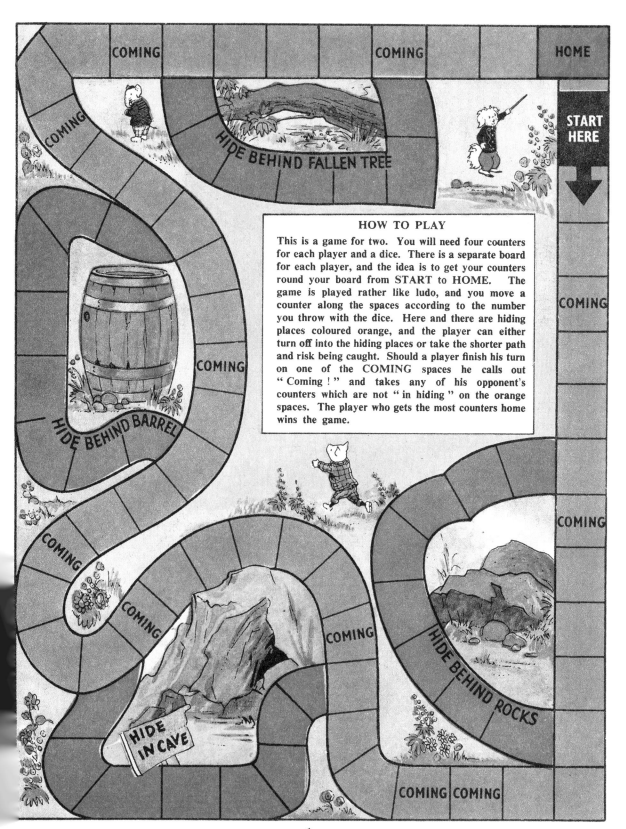

COMING
COMING
HOME

START HERE

HIDE BEHIND FALLEN TREE

COMING

COMING

HIDE BEHIND BARREL

COMING

COMING

COMING

HIDE IN CAVE

COMING

HIDE BEHIND ROCKS

COMING

COMING COMING

HOW TO PLAY

This is a game for two. You will need four counters for each player and a dice. There is a separate board for each player, and the idea is to get your counters round your board from START to HOME. The game is played rather like ludo, and you move a counter along the spaces according to the number you throw with the dice. Here and there are hiding places coloured orange, and the player can either turn off into the hiding places or take the shorter path and risk being caught. Should a player finish his turn on one of the COMING spaces he calls out "Coming!" and takes any of his opponent's counters which are not "in hiding" on the orange spaces. The player who gets the most counters home wins the game.

RUPERT'S PARTY MAGIC

Rupert's friend, the Chinese conjuror, has shown the little bear some tricks to perform at his party. Rupert dresses up as a magician and amazes his guests with the feats of "magic".

HOW TO DRESS UP

A dressing gown makes a splendid magician's robe, or you can use a coloured cloth or blanket instead.

Magician's Hat. You will also need a pointed hat. This can be made from a sheet of stiff coloured paper, which should be rolled into a cone shape as shown in the picture. Gum the edges so that the hat will keep its shape.

Magic Wand. There are two easy ways of making a wand. The one marked (a) in the picture is simply a wooden rod with a ribbon or strip of coloured paper wound on it in a spiral and gummed to

keep it firm. The wand (b) is made from a long narrow strip of paper which is first made into a tight roll and gummed at the outer end to keep it firm. Now use a pencil to push out the centre part of the roll. Then carefully pull the tip until you have a long tapering pointer.

The Mask. You can make yourself look very mysterious if you wear a mask. You need a piece of black material or thick paper large enough to cover the upper part of your face. Now fold the piece in half and cut through the double thickness, making a curved shape as shown in the picture.

CUT EYEHOLES

ELASTIC **FOLD**

Also cut out two eyeholes and make a small hole at each end to take a length of elastic. Fasten the elastic at each hole. Then try on the mask to see that it fits comfortably over your eyes and nose.

Magician's Box. Find a cardboard box large enough to hold the things for your tricks. Cover the box in black paper. Then cut out some coloured paper shapes like those shown in the picture and gum them to the outside of the box and lid. Next collect the things you need for your conjuring — some string, four empty match boxes, a few small beads and used matches, a handkerchief with a hem, a paper serviette and a walnut.

FOUR EASY TRICKS

  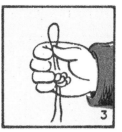 

The Magic String. (1) Show your guests a length of ordinary string. Unknown to them you have a shorter string hidden in your closed hand. (2) Crumple the long string in your hand and leave its two ends hanging at the bottom. Pull out a loop at the top, this time using the hidden short string. (3) The long piece is held by your lower fingers while the short piece is held between finger and thumb. (4) Cut the loop with scissors (the onlookers will think you are cutting the long string), then gather up the pieces in your hands. This gives you the chance to hide the cut pieces in one hand, then you can show the long string—although you have appeared to cut it in half!

  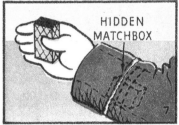

The Jumping Beads. (5) Paste coloured paper over three matchboxes, using a different colour for each. Let your audience see they are empty. Then place the matchboxes in a row, open the middle one and drop three beads into it. Close the tray and stand the box upright. (6) Now pick up each of the outer boxes in turn. When you shake them there will be a rattling sound as if the beads had moved mysteriously from box to box. (7) Here is the secret. Before showing the trick you hide up your sleeve a fourth matchbox containing a few beads, keeping it in place with an elastic band. It is this box which rattles when you pick up the empty matchboxes and shake them.

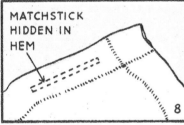  

The Matchstick Surprise. (8) You need a handkerchief with a wide hem and two used matchsticks. Before showing the trick slip one of the matchsticks into the hem. (9) Now hold the hanky open in the palm of your hand, and drop the second matchstick on to it. Wrap the hanky over the matchstick and at the same time feel for the matchstick which is hidden in the hem. Next you ask a guest to break the matchstick while it is still in the hanky and you hold the hanky in such a manner that the matchstick he breaks is the one hidden in the hem. (10) When this is done, you shake the hanky and out falls the unbroken matchstick. The broken one remains hidden in the hem.

The Vanishing Beaker. (11) Sit at a table for this trick. Place an upturned plastic beaker over a walnut. Explain that the nut has magic power and will make the beaker disappear. Now cover the beaker with a paper serviette. Make a twist at the top of the serviette, then shape it to the sides of the beaker and spread out the ends at the base. (12) Lift the serviette-covered beaker a few inches and move it towards the table edge, allowing the beaker to slip out of its cover and fall into your lap. Hold the serviette lightly so that it keeps its shape and replace it on the nut. " Now," you say, " the beaker has vanished !" and you promptly bring your fist down on the serviette, crushing it flat (13).

67

RUPERT and the UNKNOWN

RUPERT HEARS A STRANGE NOISE

" What's that I hear ? " asks Rupert Bear,
" It seems to come from over there."

Soon he hears a muttering sound,
And finds an old man on the ground.

RUPERT is strolling home one sunny morning, after playing with his pals, when he pauses beside an old oak tree and listens. " What's that noise I can hear ? " he murmurs. " It's different from anything I have ever heard before." Sure enough, a loud crackling noise is coming from behind the tree. " I must find out what it is," he says and, climbing over the fence, he gazes round to see what he can discover. By this time the crackling noise has ceased, and instead Rupert can hear someone muttering. He tip-toes forward and peers round a bush, and to his astonishment he sees a little old man sitting on the ground. The stranger is quaintly dressed in a thick coat and heavy boots and there is something rather odd about him that puzzles the little bear. Rupert runs to help the man, who is holding his head.

JOURNEY

RUPERT HELPS A LITTLE MAN

Says Rupert, " Oh, he's very small,
Not like a grown-up man at all !"

He helps the dizzy man along,
To Mrs. Bear, who says, " What's wrong ?"

Rupert asks the man what has happened and if he needs help, but the little stranger stares at him with a frown and does not seem to understand. With Rupert's help he' manages to stagger to his feet. " Why, he's hardly any taller than I am ! " Rupert thinks. " How did he get here ? What's the matter with him? " Once more the little bear questions the manikin, who mumbles one or two words in reply. " I think he's speaking in a foreign language," thinks Rupert. Then he beckons the stranger. " Perhaps you'll feel better after a cup of tea," he says. " I'll take you home with me."   The little man is still very dazed and rests heavily on Rupert's shoulder as he allows himself to be led to the Bears' cottage. " Why, who *have* you brought this time ? " gasps Mrs. Bear as the couple enter. " Is he a new friend of yours ?"

RUPERT FINDS A PUZZLING THING

" What made that noise ?   I'll go and see ! "
Says Rupert, standing near the tree.

A sudden crackling sound nearby
Makes startled Rupert leap up high.

" This thing, which gave me such a fright,
Is metal, but it's very light."

" I can't examine it down here,
So first of all, I'll pull it clear."

Rupert tells Mrs. Bear how he found the manikin. " I've no idea where he came from," he says, " and he doesn't seem to speak English. If you'll take care of him for a bit, I'll go back to that strange sound." As he reaches the tree there is another short burst of noise and the whole air shakes. Climbing the fence again, Rupert pushes through long grass. He jumps in alarm as a sudden loud crackling comes from a metal knob almost under his feet. Then the noise stops abruptly. " What was that thing ? " gasps Rupert. Making his way carefully, he peers under the leaves where a queer-looking object meets his eyes. Very gingerly he touches it, then he pushes it. " Why, it's quite light and it's metal too," he says. The noise has stopped, so he slowly pulls the object free and looks at it. " But what on earth is it ? " he thinks.

RUPERT IS WHISKED AWAY

Says Ferdy to the little pup,
" It's turned itself the right way up ! "

" What's this thing for ?   I can't decide,"
Thinks Rupert, as he steps inside.

" It's off the ground !   I didn't know ! "
Gasps Rupert, gazing down below.

The strange craft flies away so high,
They lose it in the cloudy sky.

Some of Rupert's pals, seeing him dragging the queer thing out of the bush, run forward. Before they reach him they pause and stare, for, although the little bear is not touching it, the strange cigar-shaped thing rolls slowly over until the mast is upright. "Goodness, it's hollow ! " exclaims Rupert. " It would hold me." Inquisitively he creeps forward and after hesitating he steps inside—and at that moment a violent crackling starts again.   Rupert is so intent on gazing at the metal knob at the top of the mast that is now sending out furious crackles, that he doesn't notice what is happening until he peeps over the side of the cockpit. Then he gets a shock, for the ground is now far below him. While his pals look on helplessly, the metal thing that is holding the little bear rises higher and higher and soon disappears.

RUPERT HAS A SWIFT JOURNEY

Then over sea and mountain-top,
The airship flies without a stop.

" I cannot steer this thing ! Oh dear !
It's sure to hit the wall, I fear ! "

The knobs meet with a dazzling flash,
And so the airship doesn't crash.

The manikins all stand and stare
When they catch sight of Rupert Bear.

Rupert finds himself unable to move or think after the extraordinary thing that has happened. The metal object gathers speed and streaks through the upper air at a tremendous rate over seas and mountains. "This must be a sort of airship," he thinks, " but how does it keep up ? My, it's cold up here ! " At length a grim-looking castle appears right ahead. "Oh, oh ! We're going to hit it ! " he gasps, closing his eyes tightly. But to Rupert's relief the tiny airship does not hit the building. There is a vivid flash as the metal knob connects with another attached to a tower, and Rupert is left swinging helplessly. Next moment some small figures come out and, catching sight of the little bear, they stare in blank astonishment. "Why, they're just like the man I met at Nutwood," murmurs Rupert. " Can this be his home ? "

RUPERT MEETS A MAN IN BLACK

Thinks Rupert, " Well, there's not much doubt
That these men think I should get out ! "

" It's all an accident you know,
I didn't mean to make it go ! "

" It's really not my fault, you see,"
Says Rupert, " don't be cross with me ! "

The man does not reply himself,
But takes some books down from the shelf.

At length the small people move. One of them turns off a switch and two others lift the metal thing to the terrace so that Rupert can get out. " Please, I didn't mean to make this thing go," he quavers. " Is it yours ? I know I oughtn't to have been inquisitive. And please, where am I ? " The manikins only gather round and gaze at him. " Oh dear, perhaps they don't understand a word I'm saying ! " he sighs.

" This is going to be so awkward ! " Before he knows what is happening, Rupert is hustled to another tower and confronted by another manikin dressed all in black, who seems to be the person in charge. " Oh, please don't frown at me," says the little bear. He tells the whole story and the other, making no reply, takes a couple of large books from a shelf. " What is he looking for ? " thinks Rupert.

RUPERT SEES HIS VILLAGE

The man in black then starts to look
Through all the pages of a book.

Though Rupert can't tell what they say,
He watches as the men obey.

But soon the frame is filled with light,
And then his journey comes in sight.

Then, turning round in great surprise,
"This place is Nutwood!" Rupert cries.

Still in complete silence the chief manikin studies one of the books. "Why, I can see the word 'England'," Rupert mutters. "He must have understood what I was telling him." Before he can speak again the chief strides out, and shouts orders in a strange language to the other manikins who scatter in all directions, then he hurries Rupert into an inner room. There, the head manikin places Rupert before a large frame and begins to work complicated machinery. The frame fills with light and, as Rupert watches, lovely views appear on it, showing mountains, sea and forest. "That's the sort of place I flew over on the way here," he says. "It's just like going on a journey back ! And, look—there's my very own village, Nutwood !" He turns, and at his cry, the manikin chief goes to another set of switches.

RUPERT WEARS SPECIAL CLOTHES

He wants to stay and see some more,
But he is taken to a store.

" Is this my coat ? " asks Rupert, " Good !
I do feel warm with this big hood ! "

The little people gather round,
And soon the ship is skyward bound.

" We're off ! " cries Rupert Bear, " Hooray ! "
And then the airship streaks away.

Things now happen quickly. Rupert is led away from the chief manikin, who still hasn't said a word to him, and is taken through tunnels and down stairs until his guide reaches a store. From it he brings him a heavy duffle coat with a huge hood, thick gloves and long boots to pull on over his own. Then a dark-haired manikin, similarly dressed, appears. " They're both smiling at me," thinks Rupert, " the first smiles I've seen here." The little bear soon sees why the thick clothes have been given to him. Without waiting an instant he is bustled outside and lifted into the tiny airship. His new friend squeezes in with him while other manikins crowd round. Suddenly the crackling starts again, and the little craft rises until the metal knobs connect again. Then with a loud fizzing noise the airship streaks away with its two passengers.

RUPERT LANDS NEAR HOME

And faster, faster through the sky,
The little man and Rupert fly.

Then as they land on Nutwood's height,
The other airman comes in sight.

The flier greets his friend with joy,
And hugs him like a little boy.

But just then, running up the hill,
Comes Ferdy Fox along with Bill.

Even faster than on the outward journey, the weird airship whizzes over forest, mountain and sea on the same route. At length it slackens speed and drops gently towards a hill. Rupert gives a happy shout. " This is my own village ! See, there's the church." His companion pays no attention but is already settling the ship on the grass. " Good gracious ! Look who's coming ! " cries Rupert, as they both climb out.

" It's the lost manikin ! " When the two manikins catch sight of each other they rush together joyfully. Then, forgetting all about Rupert, they dash back up the slope to the airship. " Well, of all the extraordinary people ! " says the little bear. " They must be terribly brainy and they all look old and bald, yet they scuttle about like schoolboys ! " Turning, he sees some of his friends who want to know what has happened.

RUPERT SHOWS HIS OUTFIT

" Where have you been to all the day ?
Do tell us, Rupert, please ! " they say.

" Well, if I knew, I'd tell you so !
But honestly, I just don't know ! "

" That little man was very queer,
And now he's gone away, I fear ! "

" I like those clothes they gave to you,"
Says Bill, " I wish I had some too ! "

Before the pals can reach the top of the slope, however, the queer craft has shot away. " Now Rupert," demands Ferdy Fox, " what was that thing, and where have you been ? " Rupert stares at him and then he bursts out laughing. " I haven't the least idea ! " he cries. " I couldn't understand a word anybody said, and no one told me where I was or how I got there, so I don't know anything at all ! " Mrs. Bear is waiting for Rupert as he reaches the cottage. " That visitor you brought ! " she says. " He wouldn't talk and he wouldn't eat. Suddenly he heard a loud crackling noise and rushed out of the cottage." " I thought as much," Rupert smiles. " Don't worry ! He's happy now and they've forgotten all about us—but do look at this topping flying suit they've given me after my unknown journey ! "

HOW TO MAKE
A PAPER WORK-BASKET

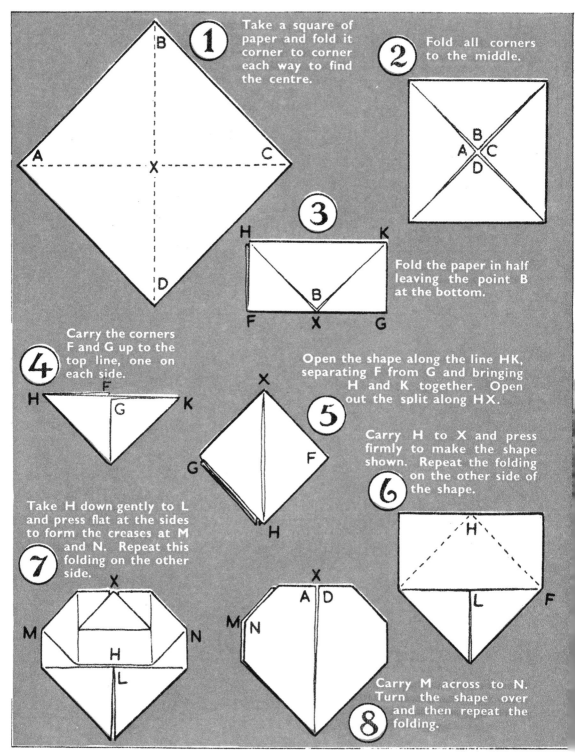

① Take a square of paper and fold it corner to corner each way to find the centre.

② Fold all corners to the middle.

③ Fold the paper in half leaving the point B at the bottom.

④ Carry the corners F and G up to the top line, one on each side.

⑤ Open the shape along the line HK, separating F from G and bringing H and K together. Open out the split along HX.

⑥ Carry H to X and press firmly to make the shape shown. Repeat the folding on the other side of the shape.

⑦ Take H down gently to L and press flat at the sides to form the creases at M and N. Repeat this folding on the other side.

⑧ Carry M across to N. Turn the shape over and then repeat the folding.

Did you notice Mrs. Bear's work-basket in "Rupert and the Unknown Journey"? This one is very much like it and you can make a model of your own simply by folding a piece of paper as shown on these pages

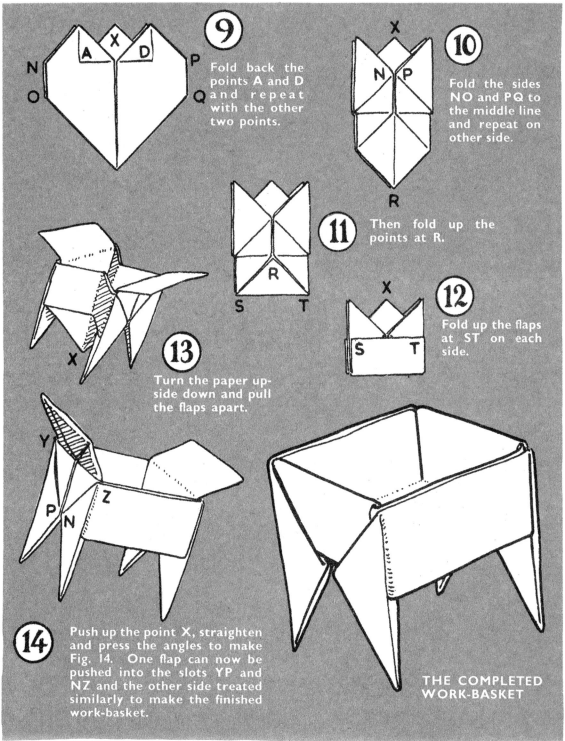

9 Fold back the points **A** and **D** and repeat with the other two points.

10 Fold the sides **NO** and **PQ** to the middle line and repeat on other side.

11 Then fold up the points at **R**.

12 Fold up the flaps at **ST** on each side.

13 Turn the paper upside down and pull the flaps apart.

14 Push up the point **X**, straighten and press the angles to make Fig. 14. One flap can now be pushed into the slots **YP** and **NZ** and the other side treated similarly to make the finished work-basket.

THE COMPLETED WORK-BASKET

RUPERT'S FAVOURITE PUZZLES

Bingo is busy at his bench, and he has no time to notice the mistakes in his workshop. For instance, look at the rocking-horse with its head the wrong way round! Study the picture carefully and see how many mistakes you can find apart from the rocking-horse. Then compare them with the list given on page 107.

RUPERT'S PICNIC PUZZLE

Rupert and Pong-Ping leave their picnic spread out in a glade while they go to a nearby stream to watch the fish leaping from the water. When they return they find that meanwhile they have had visitors and their picnic is half-eaten. "Who could have been here?" gasps Rupert. "I can't see anyone! How strange!" The culprits are not far away, however—they are hidden in different parts of the picture, so turn it this way and that and discover as many as you can. The full list of answers is on page 107.

CLUES ACROSS

1. Used in the cloud on page 94.
6. Use the letters of the answer to No. 9 and make another word.
7. How Rupert and Podgy mix the toffee on page 84.
9. A very wise bird.
10. A short name for daddy.
11. Another word for a proverb.
13. The opposite of " yes ".
15. One of Rupert's friends.
17. The third word on line four of the story on page 57.
19. One of many in the sky, on page 95.
20. Rupert floats through this on page 100.
21. Rupert wins a jug by doing this on page 44.

CLUES DOWN

1. Santa's messenger on page 91.
2. The skittles are standing in a—— on page 43.
3. Bingo uses these for boring holes.
4. To catch sight of.
5. A pond creature.
8. Podgy has a curly one.
12. How the ringmaster looks on page 45.
14. Food for horses.
16. The note between SOH and TE.
17. Mary Contrary needs a spade to do this in her garden.
18. Take ' m ' and ' e ' from " more ".
20. The second word on line five of the story on page 82.

You will find many of the answers in the picture by the crossword. The solution is on page 107.

THE NUTWOOD CROSSWORD PUZZLE

RUPERT'S BRICK PUZZLE

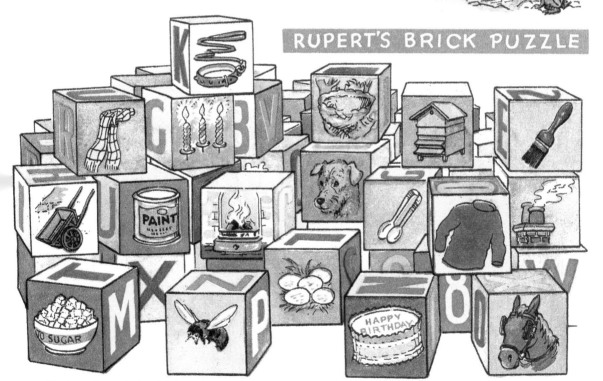

Here are Rupert's toy bricks—eighteen in all. Each picture can be paired with another, so see if you can tell which goes with which. The picture of the horse goes with that of the cart—and there are another eight pairs to be found. When you have finished check your answers with the solution on page 107.

RUPERT
and the

RUPERT DISCOVERS A SECRET

As Rupert's going out to play
A scrumptious smell is blown his way.

" What's Mummy cooking? I must see!
Why, toffee for our Christmas spree!"

CHRISTMAS is not far off and Rupert has been in the garden playing ball in order to keep warm. He is just going to look for his pals when he pauses by the open door. "There's an interesting smell coming from the house," he thinks. "I wonder what Mummy's cooking." He runs into the kitchen and, sure enough, finds Mrs. Bear busy by the stove. She is just about to lift a saucepan when she hears the little bear's footsteps. "Hullo, Rupert," she smiles, "you've caught me this time. This was meant to be a secret, but I suppose I shall have to tell you now. I'm making some toffee for you to give to your pals at the Christmas party." "How lovely! Let me stay and watch how you do it!" begs Rupert. "I have never seen toffee made!" "Oh, it is really very easy," laughs Mrs. Bear.

COUGH-DROP

RUPERT GOES TO FIND A PAL

When cooked, she hands him some to try,
And says, " I'll put the other by."

Then, running out to share the sweet,
The little bear and Podgy meet.

Rupert watches his mother while she stirs the toffee, pours it into a flat pan to cool and then breaks it up with a little hammer. " It smells gorgeous," laughs Rupert. " Well, now that it isn't a secret any longer you may as well try a bit," says Mrs. Bear, as she puts a few scraps into a piece of paper. Rupert thanks his mummy and runs outside to enjoy the little surprise. " M'm, it's scrumptious," says Rupert, as he

samples the toffee. " I must share this with somebody. I'll look for one of my pals ! " He leaves the garden and crosses a field. " Hullo, there's Podgy," he murmurs. " He will enjoy toffee if anybody will ! Hi, Podgy, you'll never guess what my mummy's made. Come and see." Podgy turns and hurries towards his pal. " Your mummy's always making nice things," he says eagerly. " What is it this time ? "

RUPERT STIRS THE MIXTURE

" It's grand," says Podgy. " I've a plan.
Let's make some. Do you think we can ? "

So up to Mrs. Pig they run
To beg the sugar for their fun.

Says she : " Here's sugar ! Butter, too !
Now, just be careful what you do."

They put the contents in a pot,
Then stir and stir until it's hot.

Rupert offers Podgy a taste of Mrs. Bear's toffee. " My, that's lovely," says Podgy. " Did your mummy really make that ? " " Yes," replies Rupert, " and I know just how to do it." Podgy pauses. " I say, that's given me an idea," he says. " Couldn't we make some for ourselves ? I'm sure my mummy would give us the things. See, there she is, with our little dog Floppy. Let's ask her. Come on, Rupert ! "

Podgy is so excited that Mrs. Pig agrees to his idea. " I have to be out for some time," she says, "and making toffee may keep you quiet so long as Rupert knows just what to do. Now I must go ; I'm already late." She bustles off while the little pals set to work cheerfully. Podgy lights a small stove, and Rupert puts the butter and sugar into a saucepan and stirs them. "That's how Mummy told me to do it," he says.

RUPERT FORGETS THE TOFFEE

And Podgy says : "Take my advice.
Let's flavour it with something nice."

He finds the mixture, pours it in.
"That's fine," he murmurs, with a grin.

They dash out when the postman comes.
"Here is the post," he tells the chums.

Oh dear, the toffee's overlooked,
The smell tells them it's more than cooked !

Podgy watches while Rupert stirs the good things. "Let's make this a special kind of toffee," he says, "so that people would know that it's our very own. I wonder what I can put in it." Getting a chair he opens a cupboard and peers inside. Then he chooses a bottle and uncorks it. "This should do," he mutters. And he pours a few drops into the mixture. Suddenly Rupert turns. "There's someone at the door," he says. Leaving the toffee, the little friends run to see who has called. "It's the postman," says Rupert. "I expect he's brought Christmas cards," says Podgy. "What a lot there are ! Come on, let's open them and see who they are from." So for the next few minutes they busily arrange the cards and think how nice they look until Podgy turns his head. "Can you smell anything queer ?" he asks.

RUPERT HAS THE FIRST TASTE

Gasps Podgy, " Ooh ! It's on the boil ! "
Oh, how they hurry, lest it spoil.

It's just a dark and sticky mess.
They chip it out in great distress.

And when to taste it Rupert tries,
It brings the tears into his eyes.

" I must," he says, " take home a bit,
To see what Mummy thinks of it."

The smell gets stronger and the two pals rush back to the kitchen. "It's the toffee !" says Rupert. "I quite forgot, we should have kept on stirring !" Podgy carries the saucepan outside. In it is a dark, sticky mess that won't pour out. "Does toffee always go like this ?" he asks anxiously. In the cold air it soon goes hard so that he can chip it out bit by bit. "Well, anyway, it *looks* like toffee," he murmurs.

Podgy asks Rupert to try the toffee first. "It's rather a queer colour," Rupert says, and pops it into his mouth. "A-ah !" he gasps. "What's wrong ?" calls Podgy. Rupert looks up with his eyes watering. "I've never tasted anything like it," he splutters. "You've invented a new kind of toffee ! May I take a piece to show my mummy ?" And, screwing up a larger bit in some paper, he races home to Mrs. Bear.

RUPERT CATCHES A MESSAGE

She says : " You've got a cough-drop here.
Don't eat a lot of it, my dear."

And then she adds, to make amends :
" Write out your list of party friends."

Down Rupert's chimney comes a card.
He seizes it before it's charred.

It's Santa's card, which says : " I fear
My presents will be late this year."

Mrs. Bear listens to Rupert's story, then she too tastes a tiny piece. " Do you know what Podgy's done ? " she laughs. " This isn't toffee, it's a cough-drop. I shouldn't advise you to eat much of it." Rupert looks disappointed, so she fetches a piece of paper and changes the subject. " Christmas is very near," she says. " So why not check the list of friends you will be inviting to your party ? " As Rupert settles by the fire to work on his party list there is a slight noise in the chimney and a thin piece of card flutters down into the fire-place. Rupert takes it to his mother. " This is queer," she murmurs. " It says : ' Santa Claus regrets that owing to circumstances over which he has no control, presents will be delayed this year '." " What long words," says Rupert, " but I see what Santa Claus means."

RUPERT HEARS ABOUT PODGY

So Rupert runs to tell this news
To all his chums, and hear their views.

They've all had cards, and all look glum.
Oh dear, why cannot Santa come?

But now comes Mrs. Pig to say :
" My Podgy's lost and gone astray."

To find him Rupert says : " I'll help ! "
Her puppy sniffs and gives a yelp.

Rupert is very dismayed at the unexpected message and he runs out to tell his friends. On the common he finds three of them, each is holding a piece of card just like his own. "So you've had one too," says Edward. "I call it a shame !" squeaks Willie. "Do you know what's happened to Santa Claus ?" asks Bill. As Rupert shakes his head Mrs. Pig and her dog Floppy come hurrying towards them.

Mrs. Pig calls Rupert aside. "My Podgy, he's gone," she says. "I left him with you, making toffee. Where is he ?" Rupert looks astonished. "We did try to make toffee," he answers, "but it turned into cough-drops. Shall I search for him ?" "Oh yes, I wish you would," says Mrs. Pig. The little dog Floppy jumps up at Rupert and sniffs excitedly. "I wonder what he wants me to do," says Rupert.

RUPERT IS GUIDED BY FLOPPY

Then Rupert takes her to the spot
Where they had scraped the toffee pot.

The dog runs sniffing with such speed
That Rupert has to drop the lead.

Then Floppy rushes to the copse,
And by the groaning Podgy stops.

"That toffee was so hot to eat!"
Moans Podgy, getting to his feet.

On their way back Rupert tells Mrs. Pig of the mistake with the toffee. "Yes, I saw my poor saucepan," she says, "and what did you do then?" Rupert leads her to the spot where he left Podgy and immediately Floppy starts snuffling busily at the grass. "He's acting like a bloodhound," says Rupert. "He must be tiring you. Shall I take him?" Mrs. Pig hands over the leash gratefully and Floppy promptly heads towards a nearby wood. The little dog pulls so hard that he drags the lead out of Rupert's hand and scampers ahead. Following as fast as he can Rupert finds him pawing at a figure seated at the foot of a tree. "Good! You've found your master," says the little bear. At the sound of his voice Podgy gets up unsteadily. "Why did I eat all that toffee? I do feel ill," he moans. "Hold me up, Rupert."

RUPERT SEES A WOODEN DOG

To Mrs. Pig they now explain
The reason for poor Podgy's pain.

Then Rupert sees, on looking back,
A strange thing on the puppy's track.

" What frightened him ? " he asks, and spies
A wooden dog ! " How strange ! " he cries.

But though he searches all around,
The wooden dog can't now be found.

Helping his pal along Rupert meets Mrs. Pig. "He's eaten all the toffee we made, he didn't know it was cough-drops," he says. "I found him lying under a tree." "Oh, my poor Podgy," cries Mrs. Pig. "Thank you for finding him, Rupert. Now I will take him indoors." Neither of them notices that Floppy is no longer there, but, on his way back, Rupert hears a noise and sees the missing dog dart out of the wood. "What frightened him?" he murmurs. "There was another animal there. It looked almost like another dog, but a queer one." Running into the wood he gets a glimpse of the newcomer before it disappears. "It's a *wooden* dog!" he gasps. "But how can it be?" He searches carefully, but he can neither see nor hear the strange creature. At length he decides to give up the search and go home.

RUPERT HAS LATE VISITORS

"Come, come!" says Mrs. Bear, when told,
"Drink this hot milk, or you'll catch cold."

To bed goes Rupert, mystified,
And hears a curious noise outside.

He looks out as a little clown
And wooden dog come jumping down.

They dance around with signs of glee,
And Rupert asks : " Who can you be ? "

Rupert gets home just before dark and tells his mother about Podgy. "He made himself ill by eating most of that toffee that went wrong," he says. "Then I saw a wooden dog in the wood, but he ran away." "A *wooden* dog? Surely not," says Mrs. Bear. "Now have your supper and go to bed." Still wondering, Rupert goes to his room. While he is taking his boots off he hears a slight noise outside his window. Rupert opens the window and peeps out. Immediately two little figures leap on to the sill. The first is the wooden dog, and, leading it by a leash, is a toy clown. They bound into the room and the clown, taking off the leash, puts it into his pocket. Shutting the window, Rupert sits on his bed and gazes at them. Then the small visitors spring up beside him. "Who—who are you ?" gasps Rupert.

RUPERT GOES ON A JOURNEY

The clown says : " This is Santa's hound.
To help dear Santa we are bound."

And when the puppy gives a yelp
It means that Rupert's asked to help !

" Remember, there's no time to pause,
We'll take you straight to Santa Claus."

So Rupert ties his boots on tight,
And all three jump into the night.

"We're from Santa Claus," the clown explains. "Did you get a note to say the presents would be late ? You did ? Well, we've been sent for help. That dog is Santa Claus's snuffle-hound. He's the only one who knows what Santa Claus wants. We thought he'd found what he needed in the wood, but now he seems certain that he wants *you*. It may seem strange, but you can always trust a snuffle-hound." The snuffle-hound won't leave Rupert's side. "There's no doubt that it's you he wants," says the toy clown. "We must take you straight to Santa Claus or else the presents may never get delivered to anybody." "But what can I do about it ? " asks Rupert. However, the clown seems so sure of what he is saying that the little bear puts on his boots again. Then all three jump from the window into the darkness.

RUPERT REACHES THE TREE-TOP

They safely land, and in a flash
Straight to the common all three dash.

There Rupert sees them climb a tree.
" Is Santa Claus up there ? " says he.

" Come up and see," the clown calls out.
" You'll be surprised, without a doubt ! "

A basket from the skies hangs down.
" Please clamber in," invites the clown.

Rupert lands safely in the garden. When he gets used to the darkness he sees his two companions hurrying out of the gate and he runs after them. The little wooden dog heads straight for the common. On the highest point he stops, the clown picks him up and starts to climb a huge tree. " Hey, where are we going ? " says Rupert breathlessly. " Come up and see," smiles the clown. Carrying the wooden dog, the clown climbs quickly and is soon out of sight. Panting, the little bear struggles upwards, until he finds himself at the very top of the tree. There, to his astonishment, he sees a round basket balanced on the high twigs. It is fastened to a rope dangling from the darkness above. The toy clown and the wooden dog are already in the basket. " Come inside, there's just room for you," says the clown.

RUPERT LANDS ON A CLOUD

There's hardly room to hold them all,
And Rupert's frightened lest he fall.

The clown then sounds a high-pitched note,
And right into the air they float.

Then through a thick white cloud they glide,
A soldier works a crane inside.

The soldier says, " I can't see how
This bear can help poor Santa now."

Rupert clambers into the basket only to find that it is too small to hold him. " Just sit on the edge of the basket and hold firmly," says the clown. " All you have to do is to cling on." He gives a high-pitched call, the rope tightens, and next moment the three passengers are swung into the air. " We're being pulled up into a cloud," gasps Rupert. There is a hole right through the cloud, and the basket just fits in as it is pulled upwards, until it emerges in clear starlight on top. " So that's what was drawing us up," says Rupert. For in front of him is a strong little crane being worked by a toy soldier. His two companions get out and walk about without fear. " This is Rupert Bear," says the clown. " The snuffle-hound insisted on bringing him. We are still wondering what it is all about. It's so strange."

RUPERT VISITS SANTA CLAUS

Now Rupert sees if he can stand
Upon the cloud. He can! How grand!

A lever's pulled, off goes the cloud,
The thrill makes Rupert gasp aloud.

They travel through the starlit night,
Until a castle comes in sight.

And Santa Claus is standing there,
Exclaiming : " Why, there's Rupert Bear ! "

The others are walking about and Rupert wonders if he can follow them. He puts one foot out of the basket and finds he can stand quite easily. " Whatever is this ? " he gasps. " It's one of Santa Claus's airships," explains the clown. " If ever you see a little cloud travelling faster than the others you'll know that it is one of these." As he speaks the toy soldier pulls the starting lever. The strange craft gathers speed and rushes through the starlit sky. Ahead Rupert sees a faint glow. It gets brighter as he draws nearer until he discovers it comes from a lovely castle built on what looks like another cloud. In a few minutes they reach it and land gently on a courtyard. Leaning over a parapet is Santa Claus looking puzzled. " Isn't that Rupert Bear ? " he murmurs. " Why have you brought him ? "

RUPERT MEETS THE REINDEER

He adds : " I simply cannot see
How you can help poor worried me."

" But follow, pray.   At any rate
I'll show you why my gifts are late."

So Rupert hurries after him,
Until they reach a stable dim.

There Santa's reindeer stand, too ill
Their Christmas duties to fulfil.

When they have all alighted Santa Claus says to Rupert, " How can you help me ? Do you know anything about reindeer ? " " Reindeer ! No, why should I ? " says Rupert. " I had a note from you, and then the clown and the snuffle-hound arrived just as I was going to bed and made me come here. And do tell me why the presents are late." " Come and I'll show you," says Santa. He guides Rupert over a bridge and then down many long staircases. At length they turn into a dim stable. " There," says the old gentleman, " these are my three reindeer, and that's why the presents haven't gone out yet." Rupert sees the long, gloomy faces of the animals, their necks wrapped with blankets, and their eyes nearly shut. " They have all caught colds and sore throats," says Santa. " They can't do their Christmas work I'm afraid."

RUPERT SHOWS HIS COUGH-DROP

Says Rupert : " It is clear indeed
A doctor is the one you need."

Just then the knowing snuffle-hound
Round Rupert starts to leap and bound.

" Perhaps," says Santa, " you possess
A thing to help in my distress."

" Well, I've a toffee lollipop,"
Says Rupert. " It's a real cough-drop."

Taking Rupert back to the main storeroom in a tower, Santa Claus sinks on to a pile of parcels. The clown and the wooden dog are already there. " If you want to cure your reindeer you need a doctor," says Rupert. " Yes, I can't see why you were brought," sighs the old man. " You'd better go home again." Rupert goes into the corridor and calls a toy soldier, but at that moment the snuffle-hound prances around him again. Santa Claus looks very puzzled. " I can't send you away when my little dog is so certain that you are wanted," he says. " Are you sure that you're not carrying something that could help us ? " Rupert's eyes sparkle. " I'm only carrying one thing," he says, " and that's a bit of home-made toffee. My mummy says it's a cough-drop." He takes it out of the paper, and hands it to the old man.

RUPERT FOLLOWS THE CLOWN

"The very thing!" old Santa cries,
And to the reindeer off he flies.

The clown says: "Rupert, follow me.
What happens we must surely see."

Right up a ladder climbs the guide,
And both soon reach the roof outside.

The clown now gives a joyful cry:
"The reindeer! See them in the sky!"

Santa studies the piece of cough-drop. "Of course, I see it all now," he says. "My little dog was right after all. Here is the secret, here in my hand!" With a rush he disappears round the corner with a delighted snuffle-hound at his heels. "What a hurry he's in," gasps Rupert. "Had we better follow?" "No, he may not want us any more," says the clown, hurrying to another tower. "But why are we going this way?" asks the little bear. For answer the clown hurries to a top room and then runs up a rope ladder to the roof. "From here we can see everything that happens in the castle," he says. "We shall soon—" He breaks off, for three dark creatures suddenly appear from below and leap happily about in the sky. "Look, the reindeer!" shouts the clown. "They're all right again! Hurrah!"

RUPERT WANTS TO GO HOME

They rush to Santa, hear him tell
How Rupert's cough-drop worked the spell.

" My reindeer now are cured," he beams,
" I'll still catch Christmas Day, it seems ! "

" Now, first of all, we'll pack the sleigh,
For there must be no more delay."

Then Santa blows his whistle clear,
And soon the reindeer all appear.

Rupert watches with delight while the reindeer prance about the sky. " My, it's a good thing the snuffle-hound found you," says the clown. " You've done the trick. Let's ask Santa Claus how it happened." They have not gone far when they meet the old gentleman. " That cough-drop of yours worked like magic," he laughs. " I broke it into three and gave a bit to each reindeer, and now they're perfectly well." Back at the courtyard Santa gives a shout and in a moment all is bustle and excitement. " Bring my smaller sleigh," he orders. " The more distant presents must be taken first." The castle guards run to obey and stack parcels in the sleigh. Santa blows a whistle and the reindeer glide down towards him. " Now, Rupert, do you want to go home with me or on my cloud airship ? " he asks with a smile.

RUPERT LEAVES THE CASTLE

And now that Rupert's task is done,
His journey home must be begun.

Back in the airship he will fly,
But first he bids the hound good-bye.

Quite soon, while gliding very fast,
They see dear Santa streaking past.

The crane and basket are at hand,
It's time for Rupert Bear to land.

"Perhaps you had better go by that same cloud airship," adds Santa Claus. "I have to go a long way round." Saying goodbye to the old gentleman, Rupert follows the clown to where the airship is resting. Soon they are on their way. "Isn't the snuffle-hound coming with us?" asks Rupert, peering over the edge. "No, his work is finished for the present," says the clown. As they sail through the night Santa

Claus and his reindeer streak past them and disappear ahead. "I say," murmurs Rupert. "Isn't this cloud airship getting very small?" "We can make it what size we like," answers the clown. "The smaller it is the faster it goes. Now look at this." As he speaks the cloud swells to a great size and stops. From under a fold the toy soldier produces the crane and then he tells Rupert to step into its basket.

RUPERT FEELS VERY SLEEPY

The little bear then holds on tight,
While he is lowered through the night.

He lands quite safely, then leaps clear,
And gasps, " Why, my own garden's here ! "

Next day he finds it hard to wake
Till Mrs. Bear gives him a shake.

Downstairs he tells of how he sped
To Santa's aid--then back to bed.

" I'm so glad we found you, Rupert," says the clown. " If it hadn't been for you nobody would have had any presents at all. Now goodbye." The toy soldier pulls a lever, and Rupert drops through a hole in the cloud. " My, how dark it is," he mutters nervously. Soon the basket bumps gently and tips him out, and is swung upwards again. " This is my very own garden ! " gasps Rupert, and he hurries in through the open window and is soon in bed. Next morning Mrs. Bear is surprised to find Rupert so sleepy. " Is anything the matter ? " she asks. " Oo, what a night I've had ! " Rupert yawns. When he goes downstairs he tells his mummy and daddy all about the cloud airship and the sky castle. " It seems almost like a dream," he says, " but one thing is certain. The cough-drop is no longer in my pocket."

RUPERT GIVES A PARTY

Says Mrs. Bear, " I've found some stuff
And made your pierrot suit and ruff."

On party nignt ne looks most gay
When all his friends arrive to play.

He tells them of his thrilling flight
To help old Santa in his plight.

With crackers gay the time goes fast,
And Rupert pulls the very last.

Rupert cannot believe that his visit to Santa Claus was a dream. " We must wait and see," says Mrs. Bear. " Meanwhile, look what I've made for you to wear at your party." She shows him a little pierrot suit with a large frill and black pompons. " How lovely ! " he cries. On the evening of his party he wears the costume when opening the door to his pals. " I've a story for you," he laughs, " and especially for Podgy." After some games Rupert's pals gather round to hear his story. Podgy gasps to hear of the snuffle-hound and the airship, and how useful his own cough-drop was. " D'you mean to say that because I made a cough-drop by mistake we shall get some presents after all ? " he asks. " That's what Santa Claus said," laughs Rupert. " Meanwhile, let's pull some of these Christmas crackers."

RUPERT FINDS A BIG SACK

Then, while a scrumptious tea they eat,
A knocking brings them to their feet.

But at the door they stand and stare,
A bulging sack is lying there.

Says Rupert, "It's for our address,
And sent to bring us happiness!"

Cries Rupert: "This is Santa's sack!
Oh, Mummy, quick! Please do unpack."

The party is going with a swing and the little pals are eating sweets and trifle when there is a knock at the front door. "Whatever can that be?" says Rupert. "Let's go and see!" They run to the door so fast that most of their caps fall off. "This is queer," says Rupert as he peers out. "The person who came has gone away again and has left a huge sack on the path. We'd better see what's in the sack," Rupert adds, "but it's too cold out here." With much excitement they drag it inside. "There's a label on it," says Bill. "See, it says 'For the small folk at Nutwood.' Whoever brought it must have known that we were all here." "I know! It must have been Santa Claus who knocked," cries Rupert. "The sack's too big to go down the chimney—that's why he left it outside the door! Look, Mummy, will you open it?"

RUPERT UNWRAPS HIS PRESENT

She tips out parcels large and small.
Three cheers! There seems enough for all!

But Rupert finds he's been left out
And wonders what it's all about.

Then comes a knocking, as before,
Why there's his parcel by the door!

And inside—look what he has found!
A dog, like Santa's snuffle-hound.

Mrs. Bear soon unfastens the sack. Then she turns it up the other way and all sorts of parcels come pouring out. "Look, they've all got names on them. I can see one for me!" squeaks Willie. The pals crowd round eagerly. Soon the parcels have all gone. "Everyone else has a present, but there's nothing for me," whispers Rupert. "Surely I haven't been forgotten." Suddenly he turns and listens. His sharp ears have heard another knock on the door and he runs to open it. Again there is no one to be seen, but on the path is a single parcel addressed to himself. Tearing off the paper, he stares in delight. "Come and look at my present," he calls. "It's a wooden dog exactly like Santa's snuffle-hound who fetched me because I had the cough-drop. This shows that my adventure was real and not a dream."

Rupert's Painting Contest

Hundreds of Grand Prizes!

Bicycles, Tricycles, Cuckoo Clocks, Wrist-watches, Tuck Hampers and Paint-boxes to be won

ALL Rupert Annual readers up to the age of fifteen can enter for this exciting contest—no matter how young you are, you have an equal chance of winning one of the splendid prizes. Colour the picture on page 106, trying your very best, and post your entry before the closing date, January 31st, 1956.

How the Prizes will be Awarded

Entries will be divided into four groups

GROUP 1. . . Boys & Girls up to 6 years
GROUP 2. . . Boys & Girls 7-9 years
GROUP 3. . . Boys & Girls 10-12 years
GROUP 4. . . Boys & Girls 13-15 years

THE PRIZES

In each of the four groups the following prizes will be awarded—

BOYS

1st . . . A BICYCLE or TRICYCLE
2nd . . . A CUCKOO CLOCK or WRIST-WATCH
3rd . . . A SURPRISE TUCK HAMPER

and paint-boxes to the 35 next-best entries in each group

GIRLS

1st . . . A BICYCLE or TRICYCLE
2nd . . . A CUCKOO CLOCK or WRIST-WATCH
3rd . . . A SURPRISE TUCK HAMPER

and paint-boxes to the 35 next-best entries in each group

Rules of the Contest

1. Colour the picture as nicely as you can with paints, crayons, coloured inks or chalks.

2. Age, skill and neatness of work will be taken into consideration.

3. Complete the entry form with your age, name and address and indicate Boy or Girl. Do not detach the form from the picture. A parent, guardian or teacher must certify that the painting is entirely your own work.

4. Send your painting together with the entry form in a sealed envelope bearing a 2½d. stamp. Insufficient postage will disqualify the entrant. Address the envelope to RUPERT'S PAINTING CONTEST, 26-29, Poppins Court, London, E.C.4.

5. All entries must be received on or before January 31st, 1956. No entry will be accepted after this date.

6. The contest applies only to readers in the British Isles.

7. Children of employees of Beaverbrook Newspapers, Ltd., are not allowed to compete.

8. The Judges' decision is final and no correspondence will be allowed. In no circumstances will competitors' entries be returned.

All prizes will be forwarded not later than March 31st, 1956. A list of prize-winners will be sent on application to RUPERT'S PAINTING CONTEST RESULT, 26-29, Poppins Court, London, E.C.4

THE PICTURE TO PAINT IS ON THE NEXT PAGE.
BE SURE TO READ THE RULES. THERE IS NO ENTRY FEE

AND LOTS OF LOVELY PAINT-BOXES

RUPERT'S PAINTING CONTEST

Rupert shows his chums some juggling tricks

ENTRY FORM *for* RUPERT'S PAINTING CONTEST

I have read the rules and agree to accept the judges' decision as final

FULL NAME..
(Print capital letters)

FULL POSTAL ADDRESS..

.... **AGE (at 31st Jan., 1956)**........

I certify that this entry is the unaided work of the above entrant.

Signature of Parent, Guardian or Teacher ....

Put a large cross to indicate boy or girl

BOY............

GIRL............

DO NOT DETACH THIS ENTRY FORM FROM THE PICTURE

Follow
RUPERT
in the
DAILY EXPRESS
every morning

SOLUTIONS TO PUZZLES

THE GIRL GUIDES' MESSAGE
(pages 6-13)

Here are the semaphore code signals together with the letters of the alphabet for which they stand. The Girl Guides' message to you reads : GOOD LUCK.

RUPERT'S FLOWER PUZZLE
(page 15)

The eight flowers are :—cowslip, poppy, buttercup, wild rose, thistle, bluebell, daisy and dandelion,

BINGO'S WORKSHOP PUZZLE
(page 80)

Here are the mistakes :—Candle upside down, clock has four hands and two pendulums, handle missing from scissors, there is no such date as February 30th, saw handle is wrong way round, spade handle is filled in, brush handle in glue-pot, odd legs on stool, gramophone handle wrong way round, sum is wrongly added, Bingo's collar and tie are back to front, box lid is hinged at front and back and handle is upside down, engine funnel is in wrong place, engine has square wheels, ruler is bent.

RUPERT'S PICNIC PUZZLE
(page 80)

Hidden in the picture are nine birds, four rabbits, three squirrels, two hedgehogs and two mice.

THE NUTWOOD CROSSWORD PUZZLE
(page 81)

Across. 1. Crane, 6. Low, 7. Stir, 9. Owl, 10. Pa, 11. Saying, 13. No, 15. Algy, 17. Do, 19. Star, 20. Air, 21. Shying.
Down. 1. Clown, 2. Row, 3. Awls, 4. Espy, 5. Frog, 8. Tail, 12. Angry, 14. Oats, 16. Lah, 17. Dig, 18. Or, 20. An.

RUPERT'S BRICK PUZZLE
(page 81)

The other eight things which go together are :—paint and paintbrush, dog and collar, cake and candles, nest and eggs, fireplace and chimney stack, bee and hive, sugar and tongs, Rupert's scarf and jersey.

Published by Beaverbrook Newspapers Ltd., Fleet Street, E.C.4 and printed by L.T.A. Robinson, Ltd.